p'tit diable numéro 2

et p'tit numéro 9

colére ou supositoire

COUDRIN– l'enfant noir

LIVRE JEUNESSE

DE 6 ANS A 17 ANS

p'tit diable numéro 2 et p'tit numéro 9 colére ou supositoire

CHAPITRE 1 bizarre

(MAMAN MAMAN)

CHUUUUUT allée dans mes

bras pas contre cette semaine
 tu reste tranquille et oui tu passe

 ton mois chez mamie LE RET

on et en NOVEMBRE en MARS
tu et chez MADELEINE PALAUD

et en DÉCEMBRE tu et chez
mamie FUSION et oui

on te laisse avec p'tit numéro 9.
MOI et grand ENCRE NOIR on

part en formation et oui
tu reste tranquille et oui en plus

tu a pas de chance tu va étre
avec l'équipe les 9 p'tit diables

pas contre pas de mauvais coup pas
contre pas de folie et de crise

colérique en plus tu et prévenu
pas de mauvaise fois non plus

ou tu fini a l'auberge PALAUD et en

plus tu va vivre pour 2 semaines
dans la maison des 4 numéro 9

et oui ils sont enfin leurs propre
logement pas contre l'équipe LOUSTI 1

 et l'équipe LOUSTI 2 on aussie
leurs logements dont beaucoup de travaille.

CHAPITRE 2 arrivé chez MADELEINE PALAUD

GHROUM

plouff il fait super froid en tous cas
ils ya pas mal de monde en ce moment

BONJOUR p'tit numéro 9 et p'tit diable
 numéro 2 allor comment ça va depuis la

dernière fois vous resté donc 1 mois

avec moi et les équipes PALAUD
je vous prévien les équipes 4 numéro 9

et les jumeaux DIALECTE sont avec
nous tous le mois papy PALAUD et

a la perchés vous allée le rejoindre
sa tombe bien ils a pas mal de

problème avec ces jambes ils
 passe sont temp debout allée l'aider

pas contre je vous prévien ce
soir vous allez dormir à l'auberge

PALAUD ET demain vous travaillerez
avec les équipes 4 NUMÉRO 9 et

l'équipes les jumeaux DIALECTE
pas contre pas de folis p'tit diable

numéro 2 et p'tit numéro 9 on vous connais

CHAPITRE 3 MADELEINE PALAUD RETOUR DE LA REUNION

GHROUM

POUFF

Alor comment ça va les équipes

KART

P TIT ANGE NOIR

LES 4 JUMEAUX MALÉFIQUES

LES 5 RAPIDOS

LES 6 DIABLOTIN

LES JUMEAUX ANGE NOIR

LES 5 DÉTACHE

LES 5 BEAUX GOSSES

LES JUMEAUX ENCRE NOIR

LES P TIT DIABLES NUMERO 1 ET 3

ALOR vous avez profité de numéro 4
et de kerivien en tous cas

vous avez été très sage
pendant mon absence pas

 contre je vous prévien

c'est vraiment très dur
de quitter ile de la réunion

sur tous qu'ils sont en
vacance actuellement

en tous cas vous resté
tranquille avec numéro 4 et kerivien.

CHAPITRE 4 démarrage des travaux de rénovation du
grenier de la maison de derrière

ALLEE les p'tit diables numéro 1
 et 3 on vous laisse téléporté

tout ce bazar dans le garage

sur la côte a droit uniquement
pas contre on vous prévien

ils faudra éviter d'exploser
les tolle en zinc et en ciment

 oui on sais elles sont
de mauvaise qualité et en fin de vie

(5 heures plus tard)

oufff voilà les nouveaux
meubles et les cloisons

en lambris on été posé
et enfin on a des cloisons

 en bois ça change et ça fait
 plus décoré de bateaux

pirates mais o moin sa
change et ça fait moins sombre.

CHAPITRE 5 plage du fozo

Bon allez les équipes

KART

P TIT ANGE NOIR

LES 4 JUMEAUX MALÉFIQUES

LES 5 RAPIDOS

LES 6 DIABLOTIN

LES JUMEAUX ANGE NOIR

LES 5 DÉTACHE

LES 5 BEAUX GOSSES

LES JUMEAUX ENCRE NOIR

LES P TIT DIABLES NUMERO 1 ET 3

je vous laisse aller à la plage
pas contre pas de bétise
et vous ne faite pas de folie sur
la plage les voisin LA famille

MIRACO et dans le
coin ils sont très insupportable

voilà pourquoi vous
dormez dans la maison
de derrière et en plus leurs
p'tit enfants sont dans

le coin donc vous resté
sur la plage du fozo évité

de rester dans le quartier.
OUI MAMIE PALAUD

aller à la plage

CHAPITRE 6 ENFIN SUR LA PLAGE DU FOZO

OUF nous voilà enfin sur la plage
en plus ils ya pas de monde.LES Équipes

KART

P TIT ANGE NOIR

LES 5 RAPIDOS

LES 6 DIABLOTIN

LES JUMEAUX ANGE NOIR

LES 5 DÉTACHE

LES 5 BEAUX GOSSES

LES JUMEAUX ENCRE NOIR

LES P TIT DIABLES NUMERO 1 ET 3

OUI les 4 JUMEAUX MALÉFIQUES

ont vous laisse faires
toutes les bêtise que vous

voulés sur la plage pas
contre pas de comédie

sur tous les P TIT DIABLES
NUMÉRO 1 ET 3 en

plus ce soir on vous

raccompagne chez vous
pas oui ils faut bien qu'on

aille gardé nos p'tit
neveux et nièces non on

dors pas chez vous
on rentre dans notre

appartement à quiberon
et oui on va enfin profiter

de notre appartement pour
nous 4 sa fait 1 super

moment qu'on a
pas eu l'appartement.

chapitre 7 arrivé chez mamie FUSION

GHROUM

BONSOIR mes loulous comment
sa va alor les équipes

KART

P TIT ANGE NOIR

LES 5 RAPIDOS

LES 6 DIABLOTIN

LES JUMEAUX ANGE NOIR

LES 5 DÉTACHE

LES 5 BEAUX GOSSES

LES JUMEAUX ENCRE NOIR

LES P TIT DIABLES NUMERO 1 ET 3

LES 4 JUMEAUX MALÉFIQUES

bon je vous donne l'autorisation
d'allée profité des source

chaude pas contre vous
reste calme, pas de crise de colère.

CHAPITRE 8 SOURCE CHAUDE

OUF nous voilà dans les source
chaude en tous cas ils ya
pas mal de touriste ils faut dit

que avec le froid et le vent
qui sont arrivé en tous

cas on aime l'hiver et l'été
pas le printemps et l'automne

ils ya pas mal de touriste
super violent et super cons

(8 heures plus tard)

Les équipes

KART

P TIT ANGE NOIR

LES 5 RAPIDOS

LES 6 DIABLOTIN

LES JUMEAUX ANGE NOIR

LES 5 DÉTACHE

LES 5 BEAUX GOSSES

LES JUMEAUX ENCRE NOIR

LES P TIT DIABLES NUMERO 1 ET 3

LES 4 JUMEAUX MALÉFIQUES

C'est l' heure de goûter

CHAPITRE 9 plage du fozo

GROURM

bon les équipes

KART

P TIT ANGE NOIR

LES 4 JUMEAUX MALÉFIQUES

LES 2 JUMEAUX BOSSEUX

ANGEVIN

LES 5 DÉMARCHES

LES 5 RAPIDOS

LES JUMEAUX ENCRE NOIR

LES JUMEAUX ANGE NOIR

LES 5 BEAUX GOSSES

LES 6 DIABLOTIN

On vous laisse sur la plage vous
 dorme chez MADELEINE PALAUD

ce soir nous on va s'occuper

des p'tit diable numéro 2 et
de p'tit numéro 9 dont on vous dit

a demain pas contre pas
de bagarre équipes

LES 5 BEAU GOSSE

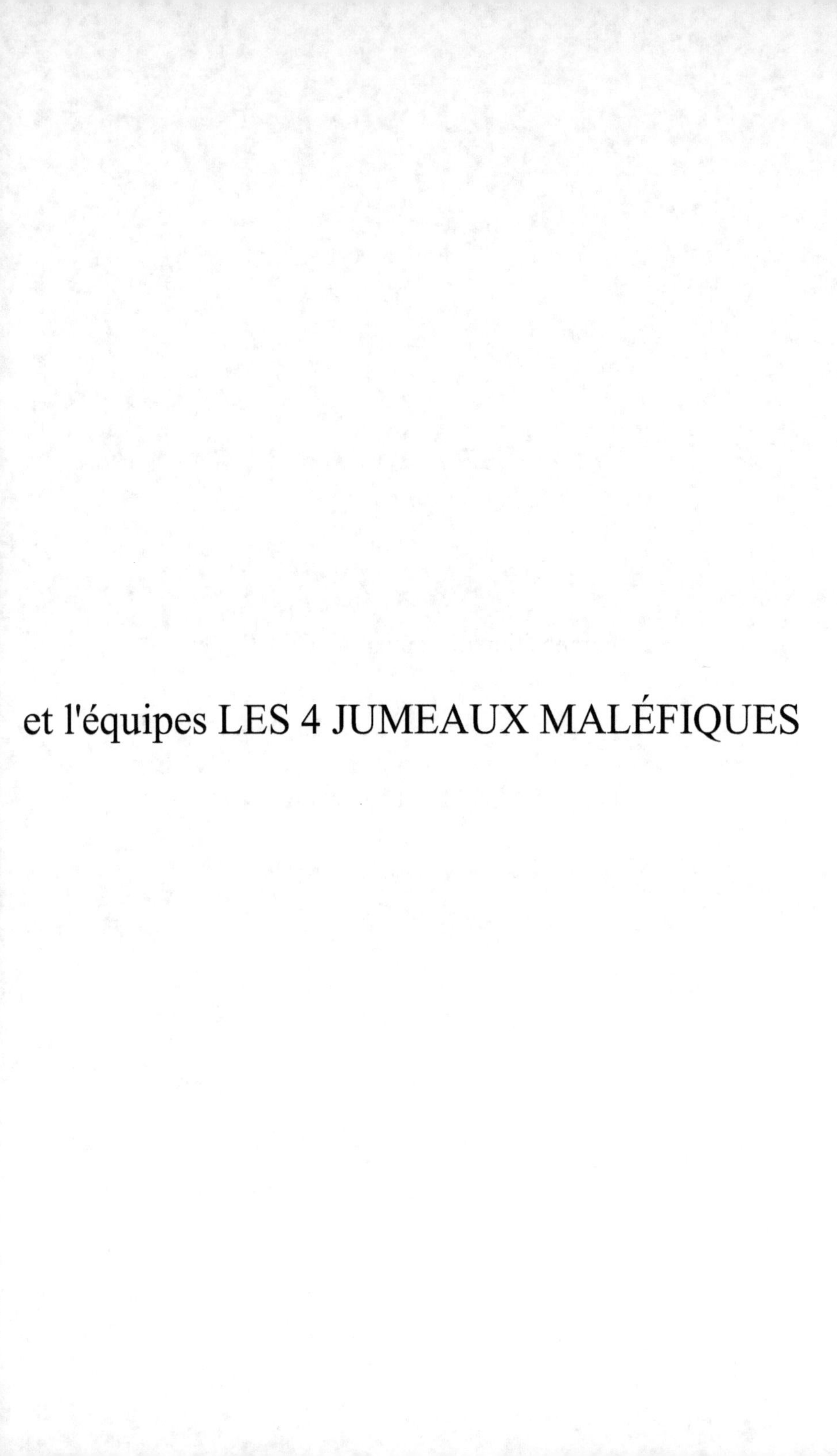

et l'équipes LES 4 JUMEAUX MALÉFIQUES

composition de couverture COUDRIN

DÉPÔT LÉGAL   15 JANVIER 2023

ISBN 97 8 24 9 44 51 7 11
PRIX
6.50€
97 8 24 9 44 51 7 11

Introduction

1001 Questions and Answers on the Christian Life

Influence of Christianity on Culture and Society

Art and Music

Social Ethics

The Place of Christianity in Interfaith Dialogue

Chapter 7: Questions and Answers

Section 1: Questions About Faith and Doctrine

- Questions about the nature of God, the Holy Trinity, and Jesus Christ.

- Questions about the inspiration and authority of the Bible.

- Questions about salvation, heaven, hell, and life after death.

Section 2: Questions About Religious Practices

- Questions about the meaning and purpose of prayer.

- Questions about the sacraments, their significance, and how they are administered.

- Questions about fasting, holidays, and other religious practices.

Section 3: Ethical and Moral Questions

- Questions about Christian ethics in daily life.

- Questions about sexual morality, marriage, and

Influence of Christianity on Culture and Society

Art and Music

Social Ethics

The Place of Christianity in Interfaith Dialogue

Chapter 7: Questions and Answers

Section 1: Questions About Faith and Doctrine

Questions about the nature of God, the Holy Trinity, and Jesus Christ.

Questions about the inspiration and authority of the Bible.

Questions about salvation, heaven, hell, and life after death.

Section 2: Questions About Religious Practices

Questions about the meaning and purpose of prayer.

Questions about the sacraments, their significance, and how they are administered.

Questions about fasting, holidays, and other religious practices.

Section 3: Ethical and Moral Questions

Questions about Christian ethics in daily life.

Questions about sexual morality, marriage, and family.

Questions about the Christian stance on contemporary social and political challenges.

Section 4: Historical and Contextual Questions

Questions about the history of Christianity and its development.

Questions about different denominations and their specificities.

Questions about Christianity in the context of other religions and cultures.

Section 5: Spiritual and Personal Questions

Questions about the development of spiritual life and a personal relationship with God.

Questions about doubts, crises of faith, and spiritual difficulties.

Questions about the role of suffering, trials, and hardships in the Christian life.

Section 6: Questions About the Church and Community

Questions about the role of the Church in the believer's life.

Questions about involvement in parish and church life.

Questions about ecumenism and Christian unity.

Section 7: Practical and Life Questions

Questions about applying Christian teachings in one's professional and public life.

Questions about raising children and youth in a Christian spirit.

Questions about managing finances and resources in line with Christian values.

Section 8: Questions About Contemporary Challenges

Questions about the role of Christianity in the world of modern technology and social media.

Questions about Christianity in the face of global issues such as climate change, pandemics, and international conflicts.

Questions about the future of Christianity and its place in a rapidly changing world.

Conclusion

Introduction

The Purpose of the Book and How to Use It

Welcome, seeker of truth, student of life, and anyone who desires a deeper understanding of Christianity – both its roots and its current expression in our complex world. This book, "1001 Questions and Answers on the Christian Life," has been created with you in mind: to serve as a guide, compass, and sometimes even a treasure map in your journey through the rich landscapes of the Christian faith.

The Purpose of the Book

Our aim is to provide a clear, accessible, and, above all, practical source that addresses a wide range of questions about Christianity. From fundamental matters of faith to the intricacies of doctrines and practices, and even everyday moral and ethical challenges – this book is designed to be a versatile tool for anyone looking to deepen their understanding and practice of Christian life.

How to Use It

"1001 Questions and Answers on the Christian Life" is designed for you to use in a way that best suits your needs. You can read it from cover to cover, use it as a reference for specific questions that pique your interest, or even as a daily guide for meditation and reflection.

For Seekers: If you're new to the faith or just curious, start by reading the introduction in each chapter. It provides context and basic information to help you understand more detailed questions and answers.

For Students: If you already have basic knowledge and want to delve deeper, focus on specific questions and answers that seem most relevant or intriguing to you.

For Teachers: This book can serve as a resource for leading discussions, Bible studies, or as supplementary material for catechetical lessons.

Each question and answer in this book is designed to provoke thought, inspire further exploration, and encourage personal reflection. Don't hesitate to jot down your thoughts in the margins, ask additional questions, or keep a journal of your discoveries.

In this journey, there are no "wrong" questions. Each one is a key that can unlock doors to a deeper understanding and a more fulfilling spiritual life. Let this book be your companion as you strive to gain a deeper knowledge of what it means to live a Christian life to the fullest and with genuine conviction.

A Brief Overview of the History of Christianity

Christianity, one of the world's largest religions, has its roots in the life, teachings, death, and resurrection of Jesus of Nazareth, who lived approximately 2,000 years ago in the region known today as the Middle East. His message of love, forgiveness, and hope, recorded in the New Testament of the Bible, became the foundation for a faith that quickly spread beyond the borders of Judea.

Early Christianity

After the death of Jesus, his disciples, known as the apostles, began the mission of proclaiming the "Good News" of His resurrection. Within the first few centuries of our era, despite persecution, Christianity thrived as an underground religion, attracting followers from various social and cultural backgrounds.

Constantine and Legalization

A pivotal moment for Christianity was its legalization by Emperor Constantine the Great in the year 313 CE in the Edict of Milan. Christianity not only ceased to be

persecuted but eventually became the dominant religion
in the Roman Empire.

East-West Split

In the 5th century CE, after the fall of the western part
of the Roman Empire, Christianity began to evolve in two
different directions: Western, centered in Rome, and
Eastern, centered in Constantinople. This led to the Great
Schism in 1054 CE, resulting in the split between the
Catholic Church and the Eastern Orthodox Church.

The Reformation

In the 16th century, a movement known as the
Reformation, initiated by figures such as Martin Luther,
led to another significant division. Criticizing some
practices of the Catholic Church, reformers aimed to
return to the original teachings of the Bible, resulting in
the emergence of numerous Protestant denominations.

Modern Development

In the modern era, Christianity continued to spread to
other continents through missions and colonization.
Today, it is practiced worldwide and encompasses a wide
range of traditions, denominations, and practices.

Contemporary Challenges

Contemporary Christianity faces challenges such as
secularization, religious pluralism, and the need for
interfaith dialogue. However, at its core, it remains faithful
to the message of its founder, Jesus Christ, and continues
to be guided by principles of love, compassion, and
community.

Main Principles of the Christian Faith

Christianity, with its rich and complex history, is built
upon several key doctrines that form the foundation of

this global faith. These principles, though subject to different interpretations depending on traditions and denominations, constitute the canonical core of the Christian belief.

Monotheism and the Concept of the Holy Trinity

The cornerstone of Christian faith is the belief in the existence of one God, who is the creator and ruler of the universe. This belief is common to many Abrahamic religions, but Christianity stands out with its unique doctrine of the Holy Trinity. God is one being who reveals Himself in three persons: the Father, the Son, and the Holy Spirit. This triunity is a mystery of faith that underscores both the unity of God and His capacity to be in a relationship with humanity.

The Incarnation of the Son of God

The central point of Christianity is the Incarnation, the teaching that God became a human being in the person of Jesus Christ. Jesus, regarded as the Messiah and Savior, came into the world to redeem humanity from sin and death. His life, death on the cross, and resurrection are the foundation of Christian hope for salvation and eternal life.

The Authority of Sacred Scripture

The Bible, composed of the Old and New Testaments, is regarded as the inspired word of God and the highest authority on matters of faith and life. The Old Testament narrates the history of the people of Israel and contains prophecies about the coming of the Messiah, while the New Testament documents the life, teachings, death, and resurrection of Jesus, as well as the early days of the Christian Church.

Sacraments as Means of Grace

Sacraments are seen as visible signs of invisible grace. Baptism and the Eucharist (Holy Communion) are the two primary sacraments recognized by most Christian traditions. Baptism symbolizes cleansing from sin and incorporation into the community of faith, while the Eucharist, also known as the Lord's Supper, is a solemn remembrance of Christ's sacrifice and a central point of communal religious life.

Christian Ethics

Christian ethics is based on the commandments to love God and neighbor, which Jesus identified as the greatest. Christians are called to live lives that reflect values such as love, forgiveness, justice, humility, purity, faithfulness, and mercy. Christian morality is not just a matter of adhering to principles but also striving for holiness in a personal relationship with God.

Mission and Evangelization

Christianity has had a missionary dimension from its inception, with Christ's command to "go and make disciples of all nations." The Church's mission is not only to nurture the spiritual life of its members but also to actively share the faith and love of Christ with the world.

Eschatology and Ultimate Hope

Christianity teaches about the ultimate destiny of humanity and the world. Eschatological beliefs include the return of Christ, the resurrection of the dead, the final judgment, and the establishment of a new heaven and a new earth, where God will reign in fullness and there will be no more suffering or death.

Chapter 1: The Beginnings of the Christian Faith

Who Was Jesus Christ?

Jesus Christ is a central figure in Christianity, not only

as the founder of the faith but primarily as its cornerstone and object of worship. His life and teachings form the axis around which Christian doctrine and practice revolve. To understand the beginnings of the Christian faith, we must take a closer look at His person, life, mission, and the lasting influence He had on the world.

Historical Jesus

Jesus, also known as Jesus of Nazareth, was born around 4 BCE in Bethlehem. His life and activities are most fully described in the four Gospels of the New Testament, which serve as the primary source of knowledge about His teachings and deeds. As a historical figure, Jesus was a Jewish preacher and teacher who mainly operated in Galilee and Judea.

The Messiah and the Son of God

In Christianity, Jesus is recognized not only as a human but also as the Messiah, meaning the "Anointed One" prophesied in the Old Testament as the savior of Israel. Christians believe that Jesus is the Son of God, signifying that He possesses a divine nature and is in unity with God the Father. This combination of divinity with human nature is crucial to understanding the Christian concept of salvation.

Teaching and Miracles

Jesus was known for proclaiming messages of love, repentance, and forgiveness. His teachings often took the form of parables—simple yet profound stories aimed at conveying moral and spiritual truths. In addition to His teachings, Jesus was renowned for performing miracles such as healing the sick, raising the dead, and feeding thousands with a small amount of food. These miracles served as signs of His divine power and compassion.

Death and Resurrection

The culmination of His life was His crucifixion, which, according to Christian belief, was a sacrifice for the sins of humanity. Jesus' resurrection, which occurred three days after His death, is regarded as the decisive proof of His divinity and the foundation of hope for eternal life. This event is celebrated every year on Easter, the most important Christian holiday.

Influence and Legacy

The influence of Jesus on history and culture is immeasurable. His life and teachings became the basis for the development of Western ethics, law, and philosophy. As a figure transcending religious boundaries, Jesus is also respected in other faith traditions such as Islam and Judaism, though in different ways than in Christianity.

What are the main teachings of the New Testament?

The New Testament is the second part of the Christian Bible, consisting of 27 books written after the life, death, and resurrection of Jesus Christ. These texts are fundamental to understanding Christianity and contain the main teachings that shape the faith and practice of Christians. Here are some of the key teachings found in the New Testament:

Love and the Greatest Commandment

One of the most significant messages of the New Testament is an emphasis on love. Jesus summarized the entire Law and Prophets in two commandments: love for God and love for neighbor (Matthew 22:37-40). Love is presented as the highest virtue that should guide all aspects of life.

Salvation through Faith

The New Testament teaches that salvation is a gift from God, available to all through faith in Jesus Christ. The letters of the Apostle Paul, especially to the Romans and Ephesians, emphasize that humans cannot achieve salvation through their own works but by God's grace, which must be received through faith.

The Message of the Gospel

The Gospel, meaning the "good news" about Jesus Christ, is a central point of the New Testament. It tells the story of Jesus' life, teaching, death, resurrection, and the promise of His return. The Gospel is a message of hope and salvation for all of humanity.

Forgiveness of Sins

The New Testament repeatedly emphasizes the theme of forgiveness. Jesus taught that forgiveness is crucial in human relationships and is a condition for receiving forgiveness from God (Matthew 6:14-15). Christ's death on the cross is presented as the ultimate means of forgiveness of sins.

Community and the Church

The apostles taught the importance of the community of believers, known as the Church. The New Testament letters provide instructions for communal life, including mutual service, sharing of goods, collective prayer, and participation in the sacraments.

Ethics and Morality

The New Testament contains many guidelines on ethics and morality. Jesus' teachings, known as the Sermon on the Mount (Matthew 5-7), include principles of humility, mercy, purity of heart, and peace. The apostolic letters expand on these topics, emphasizing the importance of righteous living, virtues, and avoiding sin.

Eschatological Hope

The New Testament concludes with the Book of Revelation, which presents a vision of the ultimate triumph of Christ and the establishment of His Kingdom. This eschatological hope is a significant element of Christian faith, offering a perspective of the final victory of good over evil and eternal life.

What were the early Christian communities like?

The early Christian communities that emerged shortly after the death and resurrection of Jesus Christ were essentially Jewish sects that recognized Jesus as the Messiah. These early groups of believers, known as "The Way," were diverse in their practices and beliefs, but they shared a belief in the teachings and mission of Jesus. Here are some characteristic features of these early Christian communities:

Establishment in Jerusalem

The first Christian community was founded in Jerusalem shortly after the outpouring of the Holy Spirit on the Day of Pentecost, as described in the Acts of the Apostles. This community was led by the apostles, including Peter and James, the brother of Jesus.

Community Life

Early Christian communities were known for their close-knit community and the sharing of goods. In the Acts of the Apostles, it is described that the believers "had everything in common" and regularly gathered for communal meals, including the breaking of bread, which later became the sacrament of the Eucharist.

Evangelization and Spreading the Faith

The apostles and other early Christians traveled to spread the Gospel and establish new communities in various cities throughout the Roman Empire. The missionary activity of the apostle Paul, who founded churches in Asia Minor, Greece, and other places, is well-documented in his letters and the Acts of the Apostles.

Meetings and Worship

Early Christian communities met in private homes, which served as places of worship. During these gatherings, they read scriptures, prayed, sang hymns and psalms, and celebrated the Eucharist.

Persecutions

Early communities often experienced persecution, both from Jewish authorities and Roman authorities. These persecutions varied in intensity and character but often contributed to the strengthening and spread of the Christian faith.

Theological Diversity

In the early centuries, there was considerable theological diversity in the interpretation of Jesus' teachings. Many early communities had their own writings, some of which were not included in the New Testament canon. These differences sometimes led to conflicts and schisms but also contributed to the development of doctrine and theology.

Role of Women

Women played a significant role in early Christian communities. Figures like Mary Magdalene, Phoebe, and Priscilla are mentioned in the New Testament as important members and even leaders in the early Church.

Development of Church Structure

Over time, as the number of communities grew, a more organized church structure began to take shape. Roles

such as bishops, presbyters (elders), and deacons
emerged to help with governance and maintaining
doctrinal and practical unity.

Chapter 2: Sacraments and Rituals

What is baptism and what is its significance?

Baptism is one of the fundamental sacraments in Christianity and is considered a rite of initiation through which a person is welcomed into the community of faith. Its significance is multi-dimensional and has deep theological, symbolic, and social roots.

Theological Significance of Baptism

In Christian theology, baptism is a sacrament that symbolizes and brings about cleansing from sin, new birth, and incorporation into the Body of Christ, which is the Church. It is an act of God's grace received through faith.

Baptism in the New Testament

The New Testament describes baptism as a ritual recommended by Jesus Himself. Before His ascension, He instructed His disciples to baptize in the name of the Father, the Son, and the Holy Spirit (Matthew 28:19). Baptism was practiced by John the Baptist, who baptized Jesus in the Jordan River, which is considered a model and example for Christians.

Symbolism of Water

Water is a central element of baptism and carries rich symbolic meaning. It represents purification and rebirth because water is the source of life and purity. In baptism by immersion, this symbolism is even more pronounced as the person is immersed in water, symbolizing death to sin and rising to new life in Christ.

Infant Baptism vs. Adult Baptism

In Christian tradition, there are various practices of

baptism. Some churches, such as the Catholic and Orthodox churches, practice infant baptism, symbolizing God's grace given regardless of personal merit. Others, such as Baptist churches, baptize only adults or older children who are capable of expressing faith and understanding the significance of this sacrament.

Baptism as a Covenant

Baptism is also seen as a covenant between God and humanity. In this context, it is a pledge of fidelity to God and a commitment to live in accordance with His commandments and the teachings of Jesus.

Social and Church Significance of Baptism

Baptism also has a social dimension as it is a public testimony of faith and includes the person in the community of believers. In many Christian traditions, baptism is an occasion for celebration and welcoming a new member into the family of the Church.

What is the Meaning of the Eucharist?

The Eucharist, also known as Holy Communion, the Lord's Supper, or the Breaking of Bread, is a central sacrament of Christianity and plays a crucial role in the spiritual lives of many believers. It is a sacrament instituted by Jesus Christ during the Last Supper with His disciples, just before His arrest and crucifixion.

Remembrance of the Last Supper

During the Last Supper, Jesus took bread and wine, gave thanks to God, and then distributed them to His disciples, saying that they are His body and blood, which will be offered for many (cf. Synoptic Gospels). Thus, the Eucharist is a remembrance of this supper and Christ's sacrifice.

Presence of Christ

In the Eucharist, according to various Christian traditions, the bread and wine become the real body and blood of Christ (transubstantiation), are considered symbolic representations of the body and blood (symbolism), or it is recognized that Christ is present in a spiritual way (consubstantiation). Regardless of the interpretation, the Eucharist is considered a sacred time in which believers can experience closeness with Christ.

Community and Unity

The Eucharist is also an act of community, uniting believers. Through shared participation in the sacrament, members of the Church are spiritually united with both Christ and each other, reinforcing a sense of unity and brotherhood.

Paschal Sacrament

The Eucharist is closely related to the Passover, the transition from death to life. Just as the Jewish Passover commemorates the liberation of the Israelites from Egyptian slavery, the Eucharist commemorates liberation from sin and death through the death and resurrection of Jesus.

Sacrifice and Thanksgiving

The Eucharist is also seen as a sacrifice – not as a repetition of Christ's sacrifice, but as a thanksgiving and memorial offering, making Christ's one-time sacrifice present in time. Many Christians believe that by participating in the Eucharist, they offer themselves to God along with Christ.

Means of Grace

The Eucharist is considered a means of grace,

strengthening and renewing the spiritual life of participants. In the Catholic tradition, the Eucharist is referred to as "the source and summit of all Christian life".

Commitment to Service

Participation in the Eucharist is also a commitment to imitate Christ, which means living in service to others and bearing witness to faith in everyday life.

What is the Sacrament of Confirmation?

The sacrament of confirmation, also known as confirmation, is a rite of initiation in many Christian traditions that more deeply incorporates the baptized into the life of the Church and strengthens the bond with the Holy Spirit. Confirmation is often seen as a complement to baptism and an important step in spiritual maturity.

Strengthening by the Holy Spirit

The primary purpose of confirmation is to impart to the confirmand a special grace of the Holy Spirit, which strengthens him in his Christian faith and life. In the Catholic tradition, confirmation is a time when the Holy Spirit bestows seven gifts: wisdom, understanding, counsel, fortitude, knowledge, piety, and fear of the Lord.

Historical Roots

This sacrament has its roots in the practices of the early Church, where baptism and confirmation were often administered together to adult converts. In later centuries, in the Western Church, these two sacraments were temporally separated, with baptism usually given to infants and confirmation at a later age.

Ritual of Confirmation

In the confirmation ritual, the bishop (or sometimes a priest) lays hands on the confirmand's head and anoints him with holy oil called chrism, pronouncing the words: "Receive the seal of the gift of the Holy Spirit." This gesture is meant to symbolize the transmission of the Holy Spirit.

Social and Personal Significance

Confirmation is also an important moment in the life of the Christian community, as it is a public testimony of faith and a commitment to live according to its principles. For the confirmand, it is a personal affirmation of faith and a commitment to be a witness for Christ in the world.

Differences in Traditions

In different Christian traditions, the practices and theology of confirmation can vary. For example, in the Orthodox Church, this sacrament, known as "chrismation," is usually administered immediately after baptism. In Protestantism, especially in Lutheran traditions, something akin to confirmation may be observed as a "confirmation of faith," but is not always seen as a sacrament in the same sense as in Catholicism or Orthodoxy.

Contemporary Challenges

Contemporary churches face the challenge of making confirmation a meaningful and thoughtful step in the life of faith, especially in cultures where religious practices are increasingly less present in everyday life.

What is the Significance of Marriage?

In Christianity, marriage is seen not just as a civil contract between two individuals, but primarily as a sacrament, a holy sign of the presence and action of God's grace. It is a union that has profound spiritual, theological, social, and personal significance.

Sacramental Nature of Marriage

In many Christian traditions, especially in the Catholic and Orthodox churches, marriage is considered a sacrament. This means that marriage is seen as a holy union, established by God Himself, and reflects the relationship between Christ and the Church, as described in the Letter to the Ephesians.

Marriage as a Covenant

In Christianity, marriage is often described as a covenant, meaning it is a commitment made before God, not just an agreement between people. It is a commitment to love, fidelity, and mutual support for a lifetime.

Cooperating with God's Plan

Marriage is also seen as a cooperation with God's plan of creation. The Book of Genesis states that "it is not good for man to be alone" and that man and woman are created to be mutual support for each other and to "become one flesh".

Personal and Spiritual Growth

Marriage is also a place for personal and spiritual growth. Spouses are called to be a source of support in difficulties, joy in good times, and help in the pursuit of holiness.

Procreation and Raising Children

In the Christian tradition, one of the purposes of marriage is procreation and raising children in the faith. The family is often called the "domestic church" because it is the first place where children learn about faith, love, and morality.

Challenges and Church Support

The Church understands that marriage can bring challenges and offers various forms of support, such as marital counseling and preparation for married life. The community of believers is tasked with supporting marriages and families in their spiritual and everyday life.

Marriage in Society

Marriage also has a social significance, as the fundamental social unit and the place where values and attitudes of future generations are shaped.

Aspects of Married Life in a Christian Context

Communication in Marriage

Communication is considered a key element of a healthy marriage. In Christianity, open and honest communication between spouses is often seen as a reflection of communication between God and humans. Spouses are encouraged to share their thoughts, feelings, hopes, and fears in a spirit of love, respect, and mutual understanding.

Sexuality

Sexuality in Christian marriage is viewed as a gift from God, meant to serve the expression of love, mutual closeness, and openness to life. Sexuality is considered something that should be reserved for marriage and is celebrated as an expression of marital unity and cooperation with God's plan for procreation.

Parenting

Parenting is often seen as a natural and desirable extension of marital love. Raising children in faith, teaching them values and morality, is regarded as one of the most important tasks of Christian parents. The family as the "domestic church" is the place where children first experience love, teaching, and religious practice.

Marital Challenges

Challenges such as conflicts, financial problems, illnesses, or differences in child-rearing are an integral part of married life. Christianity teaches that these difficulties can be opportunities for growth and deeper union if they are approached with faith and trust in God's help.

Marriage Dissolutions and Divorce

The Christian Church understands that some marriages may experience serious difficulties, sometimes leading to separation or divorce. In such situations, many churches offer spiritual and practical support while maintaining the teaching of the sanctity of marriage. In the Catholic Church, there is a process of marriage annulment, which is a way to recognize whether a union was a valid sacrament.

Church Support

The Church offers various forms of support for marriages, including preparation for married life, counseling, marriage retreats, support groups, and other programs aimed at strengthening marital bonds.

Role of Prayer

Prayer is considered an essential element of marital life. Spouses are encouraged to pray together, which can strengthen their bond and help in overcoming difficulties.

Chapter 3: Prayer and Spiritual Life

What are the Different Forms of Prayer?

Prayer is a key element of spiritual life in Christianity and takes various forms that reflect the richness of tradition and personal faith experiences. Below are some of the main forms of prayer that can be practiced by believers.

Vocal Prayer

Vocal prayer is the direct utterance of words to God. It can be either individual or communal. In this form of prayer, we distinguish:

Formulated prayers: such as the "Our Father," "Hail Mary," or "Glory Be."

Free prayers: personal expressions directed to God, expressing adoration, thanksgiving, petition, or contrition.

Meditative Prayer

Meditation in Christianity involves contemplating the mysteries of faith, passages of Holy Scripture, or truths about God and His action in history. It is a time of quiet reflection aimed at deepening understanding and relationship with God.

Contemplative Prayer

Contemplation is a form of prayer where the believer seeks to achieve deep internal silence and focus on the presence of God. It is a state where prayer goes beyond words and active effort, and the person praying experiences deep unity with God.

Liturgical Prayer

Liturgical prayer is communal prayer expressed through participation in the Church's liturgy, such as the Holy Mass, the Liturgy of the Hours, or other sacraments. It is the public and official prayer of the Church.

Charismatic Prayer

In the charismatic tradition, prayer often takes the form of worship, where participants may also experience gifts of the Holy Spirit, such as speaking in tongues, prophecy, or healing.

Praise Prayer

Praise prayer focuses on glorifying God for His greatness and goodness. It is a form of prayer that expresses joy and gratitude, often through singing and music.

Supplicatory and Intercessory Prayer

Supplicatory prayer is a prayer of petition for oneself, while intercessory prayer is a prayer of intercession for others. It includes requests for health, help in difficulties, as well as prayers for the deceased.

Prayer of Silence and Listening

In this form of prayer, the believer spends time in silence, trying to listen to God's voice. It is a practice that requires patience and discipline but can lead to profound personal revelations.

Rosary Prayer

The Rosary is a form of Marian prayer that combines meditation on the mysteries of the life of Jesus and Mary with vocal prayer.

How to Develop Spiritual Life?

The development of spiritual life in Christianity is a process that involves both personal commitment and support from the faith community. Here are some key practices and disciplines that can help deepen spiritual life:

Regular Prayer

The foundation of spiritual life is regular prayer. Establishing a daily rhythm of prayer, whether in the morning, evening, or throughout the day, helps maintain constant communication with God.

Study of Holy Scripture

Reading and meditating on God's Word is essential for spiritual growth. Bible study, both individually and in a group, allows for a better understanding of God's message and its application in life.

Participation in Liturgy

Regular participation in liturgy and sacraments, especially the Eucharist, strengthens the relationship with God and the community of believers, and is a source of grace and spiritual nourishment.

Fasting and Abstinence

Fasting and other forms of abstinence can help purify spiritual life, teaching self-discipline and opening the heart to God's action.

Spiritual Reading

Reading spiritual classics, works of saints and theologians can be inspiring and provide new perspectives on faith and spiritual practice.

Retreats and Solitude

Participating in retreats or solitude offers an opportunity for deeper reflection and prayer away from daily activities.

Charitable Activity

Serving others is not only an expression of love for one's neighbor but also a way to experience and practice faith in action.

Faith Community

Engaging in the life of the faith community, such as prayer groups, parish communities, or church movements, can provide support and encouragement on the spiritual journey.

Spiritual Leadership and Mentoring

Seeking spiritual guidance, whether through a relationship with a clergy member, an experienced spiritual mentor, or participation in formation groups, can help navigate spiritual life.

Contemplative Practices

Practices such as Christian meditation, contemplation, or mindfulness practices can help achieve a deeper awareness of God's presence.

Spiritual Journaling

Keeping a spiritual journal, where one records thoughts, prayer experiences, and spiritual insights, can help in understanding and appreciating the path God leads one on.

Evangelization and Testimony

Sharing one's faith with others can be a powerful tool for spiritual growth, as through testimony and evangelization, believers themselves become more committed to their convictions.

What is the Significance of Meditation and Contemplation in Christianity?

Meditation and contemplation are deeply rooted in the Christian spiritual tradition and play a crucial role in developing the inner life of believers. These spiritual practices are pathways to a deeper understanding of God, oneself, and the world around us.

Christian Meditation

Meditation in Christianity often focuses on reflecting upon the Holy Scriptures, especially through a prayerful reading known as lectio divina. This practice involves several stages: reading (lectio), meditation (meditatio), prayer (oratio), and contemplation (contemplatio). Meditation is a time when believers actively ponder the Word of God, seeking personal messages and guidance for living.

In Christian meditation, the aim is to pause in the daily rush, focus attention on God's word, and allow its truths to permeate the heart and mind. It's a process in which believers reflect on God's love, His promises, commandments, and plan of salvation. This meditation can take the form of deep reflection on a specific Bible passage, contemplation of the mysteries of faith, or pondering God's works in nature and history.

Contemplation

Contemplation in Christianity is even more internal and passive than meditation. It is a state of deep silence and peace, where the believer seeks to be completely open to the presence of God and lets Him work in their heart.

Contemplation is not about active thinking but being in the presence of God, "looking at Him with the heart," as St. Augustine put it.

In the Christian tradition, contemplation is often seen as a gift from God, not something achievable through one's effort. It is a time when prayer goes beyond words and reaches a deep communion with God that transforms the heart and mind. Contemplation can lead to mystical experiences, where the believer experiences unity with God that transcends human understanding.

Significance for Spiritual Life

Meditation and contemplation are of great importance to spiritual life, as they help believers focus on God's word and presence, which is essential for a deep prayer life. Through these practices, believers can experience a transformation of the heart, leading to a deeper love for God and others, greater humility, patience, and other fruits of the Holy Spirit.

Moreover, meditation and contemplation can be an antidote to the stress and hustle of modern life. They teach quietness, focus, and being present in the moment, which has beneficial effects not only on spiritual life but also on emotional and physical health.

Integration into Daily Life

Meditation and contemplation are not detached from daily life; on the contrary, they aim to sanctify it. Through these practices, believers learn to see everything in God's light and respond to daily events with more love and understanding. They are tools that help believers live more consciously and responsibly as God's children in the world.

Chapter 4: Christian Ethics and Morality

What Does the Bible Say About Marriage and Parenthood?

The Bible presents marriage and parenthood as institutions established by God, having key significance for social and spiritual life. They are deeply rooted in Christian ethics and reflect God's plan for humanity.

Marriage in Biblical Teaching

God's Plan for Marriage: In the Book of Genesis (Genesis 2:24), we read, "a man shall leave his father and mother and be joined to his wife, and they shall become one flesh." Marriage is depicted as a sacred union between a man and a woman, intended for mutual support, love, and procreation.

Fidelity and Unity: Marriage is a place of fidelity and indissolubility. In the Gospel of Matthew (Matthew 19:6), Jesus says, "Therefore what God has joined together, let no one separate." Marital fidelity is the foundation of family life.

Marital Love: In the Letter to the Ephesians (Ephesians 5:25-33), St. Paul compares marital love to Christ's love for the Church, calling husbands to love their wives "as Christ loved the Church." Thus, marriage is an image of God's love.

Parenthood in Biblical Teaching

Heritage and Blessing: Children are portrayed as a heritage from the Lord and a blessing (Psalm 127:3-5). Parenthood is therefore not just a biological act of procreation but also a spiritual vocation to raise children in faith and love.

Raising in Discipline and Instruction of the Lord: In the Letter to the Ephesians (Ephesians 6:4), Apostle Paul urges parents to bring up their children "in the discipline and instruction of the Lord." This means that parents have a responsibility for the spiritual development and moral shaping of their children.

Example and Teaching: The Bible emphasizes the role of parents as the first and most important teachers of their children. In the Book of Proverbs (Proverbs 22:6), we read, "Train up a child in the way he should go; even when he is old he will not depart from it." Parents are called to be examples and to pass on values.

Ethical and Moral Challenges

Divorces and Separations: The Bible speaks of the difficulties and challenges associated with marriage, including divorces. However, Biblical teaching emphasizes that divorce is contrary to God's plan for marriage and should be the last option after exhausting all possibilities for reconciliation and repair of the relationship.

Role of Parents in the Modern World: Contemporary challenges, such as the impact of technology, cultural diversity, and social changes, pose new questions for parents regarding child-rearing. The Bible provides principles that can help parents navigate these challenges while maintaining fidelity to Christian values.

What is the Christian Approach to Professional Ethics?

Christian professional ethics are based on principles derived from Biblical teaching, emphasizing honesty, responsibility, service, and love for one's neighbor. These values are not only benchmarks for personal life but also shape the approach to professional work.

Integrity and Righteousness

Truthfulness: In the Book of Proverbs (Proverbs 12:22), it is said, "Lying lips are an abomination to the LORD, but those who act faithfully are his delight." Christian professional ethics promote being truthful in every aspect of work.

Justice: The Bible calls for fair treatment of others, which in a professional context means justly compensating workers (Colossians 4:1) and conducting business fairly.

Responsibility and Diligence

Care for Entrusted Tasks: The Parable of the Talents (Matthew 25:14-30) emphasizes the value of responsibility and utilizing entrusted resources. In professional work, this means conscientiously performing duties and striving for excellence.

Diligence: In the Book of Proverbs (Proverbs 6:6-8), one is called to imitate the ant in her diligence. Christian professional ethics value effort and commitment to work.

Service and Care for Others

Service as a Calling: Work is seen not only as a means to earn a living but as a calling to serve others and society (Ephesians 4:28).

Empathy and Compassion: Christian professional ethics encourage empathy in the workplace, meaning concern for the well-being of co-workers and clients (Galatians 6:2).

Integrity and Alignment with Values

Alignment with Values: Believers are called to live according to evangelical values, which means avoiding ethical compromises in work (Romans 12:2).

Resistance to Corruption: Christianity condemns all forms of corruption and dishonesty, calling for maintaining integrity even in the face of temptation (Hebrews 13:18).

Balanced Lifestyle

Balancing Work and Rest: The Bible speaks about the importance of rest, which in professional practice means caring for a balance between work and personal life (Exodus 20:8-11).

Attitude of Continuous Development

Learning and Development: Christian professional ethics promote continuous learning and personal development as a way to serve God and others in increasingly better ways (Colossians 3:23).

How to Deal with Temptations and Sins?

Dealing with temptations and sins is a central element of Christian ethics and morality. In Christianity, temptation is not a sin in itself; sin occurs when one succumbs to temptation. Here are some biblical and theological guidelines on dealing with temptations and sins:

Acknowledging Human Weakness

Humility: The first step is recognizing that everyone is susceptible to temptations and no one is free from sin (Romans 3:23). Humility allows for a realistic view of one's limitations and the need for God's grace.

Seeking God's Help

Prayer: Jesus taught His disciples to pray not to fall into temptation (Luke 22:40). Regular prayer strengthens the spirit and helps resist temptations.

Sacraments: In Christianity, sacraments, especially the Sacrament of Penance and the Eucharist, are sources of grace that assist in combating temptations and healing from sin.

Knowledge of God's Word

Bible Study: Knowledge of the Holy Scriptures is essential as it provides guidance and strength to fight against temptations. The Psalmist says, "Your word is a lamp to my feet and a light to my path" (Psalm 119:105).

Avoiding Occasions of Sin

Vigilance: Christian ethics teach to avoid situations that might lead to sin (Colossians 3:5). This could mean avoiding certain places, situations, or even company that might expose one to temptations.

Spiritual Practices

Fasting and Asceticism: These practices help in strengthening the will and rejecting unnecessary attachments, thereby enhancing the ability to resist temptations.

Contemplation: Reflecting on the life of Christ, His suffering, and love for humanity can inspire to reject sin and follow His example.

Community and Support

Faith Community: Participation in the life of the Church and small prayer groups can provide support and encouragement in combating temptations.

Spiritual Leadership: Seeking advice and support from clergy or experienced spiritual mentors can assist in identifying and overcoming temptations.

Practical Steps

Replacing Bad Habits with Good Ones: Instead of succumbing to bad habits, one can seek healthy alternatives that bring true joy and fulfillment.

Engagement in Constructive Activities: Active participation in church activities, volunteering, or other forms of service can distract from temptations and channel energy into positive actions.

Forgiveness and Healing

Forgiving Oneself: Understanding that God is merciful and ready to forgive allows for rebuilding after a fall and continuing the spiritual journey without discouragement.

Regular Use of the Sacrament of Penance: The Sacrament of Penance is a place to obtain forgiveness and grace to combat sin.

Chapter 5: Churches and Denominations

What are the Main Differences Between Catholics and Protestants?

Theological Differences

Authority in the Church: Catholicism is based on three pillars of authority: Scripture, Tradition, and the Magisterium of the Church. The Pope and bishops, as successors of the apostles, have the authority to interpret Scripture and Tradition. Protestants, on the other hand, often rely solely on Scripture as the highest authority, rejecting external church authorities as equal sources of truth.

Justification and Salvation: Catholicism teaches that justification is a process in which man cooperates with God's grace through faith and good works. Protestants, especially those from Lutheran and Calvinist traditions, believe that justification is an act of God's grace received through faith, and good works are a fruit of this faith, not its condition.

Structural and Practical Differences

Church Hierarchy: Catholicism has a strongly organized, hierarchical church structure, with the Pope as the head of the Church. In Protestantism, church structures are more varied, from episcopal (with bishops), through presbyterian (assemblies of elders), to congregational (independent local churches).

Veneration of Saints and Mary: In Catholicism, there is a practice of asking saints and Mary for intercession, which is an expression of the belief in the communion of saints. In Protestantism, especially in its more evangelical and reformed variants, prayer is directed solely to God, and the role of saints is significantly less emphasized.

Differences in Moral Teaching

Clerical Marriage: In the Western Catholic Church, priests are required to observe celibacy, symbolizing total dedication to God's service. In Protestantism, clergy can marry, which is seen as a natural part of life and ministry.

Birth Control: Catholicism traditionally teaches that artificial methods of contraception are morally unacceptable, promoting natural family planning methods. Many Protestants accept various forms of birth control, emphasizing responsibility and freedom of conscience in these decisions.

Differences in Understanding the Eucharist

Transubstantiation vs. Symbolism: Catholics believe that during the Eucharist, bread and wine become the actual Body and Blood of Christ through transubstantiation, though they retain their physical properties. Many Protestants, including Lutherans and Anglicans, believe in some form of real presence of Christ in the Eucharist, but understand it differently than Catholics. Other Protestant groups, like Baptists or Pentecostals, may view the Eucharist as a symbolic commemoration of the Last Supper.

Differences in Approach to the Bible

Interpretation of Scripture: Catholicism encourages reading and interpreting the Bible in light of Tradition and the teaching of the Church. In Protestantism, there is a greater emphasis on individual study of Scripture and personal interpretation, although within specific denominations there may be guidelines for understanding key doctrines.

Differences in Approach to Tradition

Role of Tradition: In Catholicism, Tradition (with a

capital "T") is seen as a parallel source of God's revelation alongside Scripture. In Protestantism, especially in its reformed variants, tradition (with a lowercase "t") is treated as historical context, which can be helpful but does not hold the same authority as Scripture.

What is the Orthodox Church?

The Orthodox Church, often referred to as Orthodoxy, is one of the oldest Christian traditions in the world. It is characterized by a deep respect for Tradition, passed down from generation to generation, forming an integral part of life and worship. Here are some key aspects of the Orthodox Church:

History and Development

East-West Schism: Orthodoxy separated from the Western Church as a result of the Great Schism in 1054, which was a split between the Roman Catholic and Orthodox Churches, mainly due to theological and cultural differences, as well as disputes over power and jurisdiction.

Autocephaly: Orthodox Churches are organized in an autocephalous manner, meaning each national Orthodox Church has its own head (e.g., a patriarch, archbishop) and governs itself independently, though all are united in faith and sacraments.

Theology and Spirituality

Theocentrism: Orthodoxy places a strong emphasis on the mystery of God and His incomprehensible essence. Orthodox spirituality is deeply rooted in seeking union with God, known as theosis, or the process of becoming like God through grace.

Icons: In Orthodoxy, icons are not just religious art but are considered "windows to heaven" that enable the faithful to have spiritual encounters with holy figures. Icons are objects of veneration but not worship, which is due to God alone.

Liturgy and Sacraments

Liturgy: The Orthodox liturgy is rich in symbols and rituals intended to reflect the beauty and holiness of heaven. The liturgy is usually longer and more ornate than in most Western traditions.

Sacraments: Similar to Catholicism, Orthodoxy recognizes seven sacraments, including the Eucharist, baptism, confirmation (in Orthodoxy known as chrismation), confession, marriage, holy orders, and anointing of the sick.

Practices and Traditions

Fasting: Orthodoxy is known for its rigorous fasting practices, which include many days throughout the year and are part of spiritual discipline.

Jesus Prayer: This is a central prayer practice in Orthodoxy, involving the continuous repetition of Jesus' name for deep contemplation and heart prayer.

Role of the Clergy

Celibacy: Unlike the Catholic Church, in Orthodoxy, parish priests may be married before ordination, but bishops are usually chosen from among monks who are celibates.

Apostolic Succession: Like Catholics, Orthodox maintain that their bishops are in an unbroken line of apostolic succession, ensuring the validity of their sacraments and teachings.

Challenges and Modernity

Ecumenism: Orthodoxy engages in ecumenical dialogue, though often with more caution than some other Christian traditions, emphasizing the necessity of preserving true faith and practices.

Globalization: Facing globalization and migration, Orthodoxy is challenged with maintaining its identity and traditions in a diverse and changing world.

What are the Lesser-Known Christian Denominations?

Christianity, being one of the world's largest religions, is also one of the most diverse, with many smaller denominations and groups that differ doctrinally, liturgically, and in spiritual practices. Here are some examples of lesser-known Christian denominations:

Anabaptists

Characteristics: Anabaptists are known for their radical approach to Christianity, which includes pacifism, voluntary adult baptism, and separation from the state.

Examples: Mennonites, Amish, Hutterites.

Anglicanism

Characteristics: While the Anglican Church is a large denomination, there are many smaller Anglican groups that have split off for various reasons, often related to the liberalization of mainstream Anglicanism.

Examples: Traditional Anglican Church, Continuing Churches.

Adventists

Characteristics: Adventists are known for their unique emphasis on the imminent return of Christ (Advent) and observing the Sabbath as a holy day.

Examples: Seventh-day Adventists, Reform Adventists.

Pentecostalism and Charismatic Movement

Characteristics: Although some of these movements are quite large, there are many smaller Pentecostal and Charismatic groups that emphasize the workings of the Holy Spirit, spiritual gifts such as speaking in tongues, prophecy, and healing.

Examples: Church of God, Assemblies of God, independent Charismatic churches.

Restorationism

Characteristics: Restorationist movements aim to restore what they see as the original Christianity of the first century.

Examples: The Church of Jesus Christ of Latter-day Saints (Mormons), Jehovah's Witnesses, Church of Christ.

Quakers (Religious Society of Friends)

Characteristics: Quakers are known for their simplicity, pacifism, and inner enlightenment through the "Inner Light".

Examples: Conservative Friends, Liberal Friends.

Independent and House Churches

Characteristics: These groups often arise from a desire for more authentic Christian living outside the structures of large denominations.

Examples: House churches, independent Christian communities.

Oriental Orthodox Churches

Characteristics: While not "lesser" in a global sense, in regions like North America and Europe, Oriental Orthodox Churches are in the minority.

Examples: Coptic Orthodox Church, Syriac Orthodox Church.

Old Catholic Churches

Characteristics: Old Catholics split from the Roman Catholic Church due to disagreements with the doctrines established at the First Vatican Council, particularly the infallibility of the pope.

Examples: Union of Utrecht of the Old Catholic Churches.

Diversity in Christianity

It's important to note that each of these groups has its own unique identity and practices, which can vary significantly even within a given tradition. Some may be more conservative or liberal in their interpretations of Christian doctrine and ethics. All these groups contribute to the rich mosaic of Christian experience and express the diversity of ways in which people understand and live out their faith.

Chapter 6: Christianity in Today's World

What are the Biggest Challenges for Christians in the 21st Century?

Secularization and Relativism

Understanding and Response: Christians must understand how to live their faith in a world that often rejects absolute moral standards and truths. This requires them to not only defend their beliefs but also present Christianity in a way that is accessible and convincing to those with a secular worldview.

Examples of Actions: Development of Christian apologetics, intercultural dialogues, creating spaces for Christian art and literature that can speak to contemporary cultures.

Religious Pluralism and Interfaith Dialogue

Understanding and Response: The challenge is finding a balance between remaining faithful to Christian doctrine and being open to other religions. This requires a deep knowledge of one's own faith and an understanding of other religious traditions.

Examples of Actions: Participation in interfaith working groups, conferences, joint social projects promoting peace and understanding.

Morality and Social Ethics

Understanding and Response: Christians are called to engage in social and political debates on ethics, presenting a perspective based on Gospel values. This requires wisdom, compassion, and courage.

Examples of Actions: Education and formation of conscience, involvement in social initiatives, supporting pro-life organizations, activities in the area of marriage and family protection.

Technology and Social Media

Understanding and Response: Christians need to learn how to use new media in an ethical and constructive way, utilizing them for evangelization and community building.

Examples of Actions: Creating digital content that is attractive, authentic, and theologically sound; training in safe internet usage.

Poverty and Social Injustice

Understanding and Response: Christianity has a long history of engaging in helping the needy and fighting injustice. Contemporary challenges require Christians to respond both locally and globally.

Examples of Actions: Development and support for aid and development programs, engagement in fair trade, activities for human rights.

Ecology and Environmental Protection

Understanding and Response: Christians are called to reflect on how their faith informs their responsibility for the environment and to act to protect it.

Examples of Actions: Promoting a sustainable lifestyle, support for ecological initiatives in churches, ecological education based on Christian doctrine of creation.

Persecution and Religious Freedom

Understanding and Response: Persecution is a brutal reality for many Christians. The challenge is to raise awareness and act for religious freedom worldwide.

Examples of Actions: Information campaigns, support for refugees and victims of persecution, political lobbying for religious freedom.

Internal Divisions and Christian Unity

Understanding and Response: The challenge is to build unity in diversity, which requires dialogue, mutual understanding, and cooperation among different Christian traditions.

Examples of Actions: Ecumenical prayer initiatives, joint social projects, theological dialogue aimed at mutual understanding and respect.

How Does Christianity Influence Culture and Society?

Christianity, as one of the major forces shaping the West, continues to exert a significant influence on culture and society, even in an increasingly secularized world. Here are some key areas where Christianity impacts:

Art and Literature

Understanding and Response: Christianity has inspired artists and writers for centuries. Contemporary Christianity continues this tradition, promoting art and literature that reflect Christian values and perspectives.

Examples of Actions: Supporting Christian artists, sacred art festivals, literary publications with a Christian message, competitions for young creators.

Ethics and Law

Understanding and Response: Christian ethics influence debates on human rights, social justice, and legislation. Christian lawyers and politicians often base their views on values derived from their faith.

Examples of Actions: Christian think tanks, seminars and conferences on public ethics, engagement in the legislative process.

Education and Science

Understanding and Response: Christianity has a long history of promoting education and scientific research. Many contemporary universities and schools have Christian roots and continue to promote values such as the pursuit of truth and community service.

Examples of Actions: Christian colleges and educational programs, grants and scholarships for young scientists, scientific conferences with a Christian perspective.

Media and Communication

Understanding and Response: Christianity uses media to communicate its message, educate the faithful, and influence society. Christian radio and TV stations, publishers, and online platforms are tools for evangelization and shaping public opinion.

Examples of Actions: Christian TV and radio programs, online portals, social media campaigns, mobile apps with Christian content.

Family and Community

Understanding and Response: Christianity promotes family and community values, encouraging the building of strong, mutually supportive communities. Churches often offer support programs for marriages, parents, and youth.

Examples of Actions: Workshops and courses for married couples, educational programs for parents, youth camps and groups, initiatives supporting families in need.

Economy and Work

Understanding and Response: Christian work ethics and corporate social responsibility are part of a broader discussion about the role of faith in the economy. Christians are encouraged to conduct business ethically and treat workers fairly.

Examples of Actions: Christian business networks, ethical investments, career development programs based on Christian values.

Politics and Civil Society

Understanding and Response: Christians are encouraged to actively participate in public life, promoting values such as justice, peace, and care for the poor.

Examples of Actions: Engagement in non-governmental organizations, Christian political parties, initiatives for peace and justice.

Culture and Traditions

Understanding and Response: Christianity shapes cultural traditions and holidays that are celebrated by many, even non-practicing Christians. These traditions can serve as bridges to deeper understanding and practicing of faith.

Examples of Actions: Public celebrations of Christian holidays, Christian culture festivals, education about Christian traditions.

Chapter 7: Questions and Answers

Section 1: Questions on Faith and Doctrine

- Questions about the nature of God, the Holy Trinity, and Jesus Christ.

- Questions concerning the inspiration and authority of the Bible.

- Questions about salvation, heaven, hell, and life after death.

Section 2: Questions on Religious Practices

- Questions on the meaning and purpose of prayer.

- Questions about the sacraments, their significance, and how they are administered.

- Questions on fasting, holidays, and other religious practices.

Section 3: Ethical and Moral Questions

- Questions concerning Christian ethics in everyday life.

- Questions about sexual morality, marriage, and family.

- Questions regarding the Christian stance towards contemporary social and political challenges.

Section 4: Historical and Contextual Questions

- Questions about the history of Christianity and its development.

- Questions on various denominations and their specificities.

- Questions about Christianity in the context of other religions and cultures.

Section 5: Spiritual and Personal Questions

- Questions about the development of spiritual life and personal relationship with God.

- Questions concerning doubts, crises of faith, and spiritual difficulties.

- Questions on the role of suffering, trials, and difficulties in Christian life.

Section 6: Questions on the Church and Community

- Questions about the role of the Church in a believer's life.

- Questions concerning involvement in parish and church life.

- Questions about ecumenism and Christian unity.

Section 7: Practical and Life Questions

- Questions about applying Christian teachings in professional and public life.

- Questions concerning raising children and youth in the Christian spirit.

- Questions about managing finances and resources in a way consistent with Christian values.

Section 8: Questions on Contemporary Challenges

- Questions about the role of Christianity in the world of modern technology and social media.

- Questions concerning Christianity in the face of global issues such as climate change, pandemics, and international conflicts.

- Questions about the future of Christianity and its place in a rapidly changing world.

Section 1: Questions on the Nature of God

Question: How does Christianity define God?

Answer: Christianity defines God as almighty, omniscient, eternal, infinite, and a personal spirit, who is the creator and sustainer of the universe.

Question: Can God be known by humans?

Answer: Yes, Christianity teaches that God has revealed Himself to humans through creation, history, Scripture, and most fully through Jesus Christ.

Question: How does God communicate with humans?

Answer: God communicates with humans through revelation, which can take the form of inspiration, prophecy, Scripture, and the internal working of the Holy Spirit.

Question: Is God a person?

Answer: Yes, Christianity describes God as a personal being, capable of thinking, will, emotions, and relationships.

Question: What is the omnipotence of God, and does it have any limits?

Answer: The omnipotence of God means that He is capable of doing everything that is logically possible and is not limited by anything other than His own nature.

Question: Does God change over time?

Answer: No, Christianity teaches about the immutability of God, which means His nature, character, and will remain unchanged.

Question: What are the attributes of God according to Christian doctrine?

Answer: The attributes of God include His holiness, justice, love, mercy, omniscience, omnipresence, eternity, and immutability.

Question: Is God present in everything that exists?

Answer: Yes, Christianity teaches about the omnipresence of God, which means that He is present in everything, but not identical with it.

Question: Is God the only one, or are there other gods?

Answer: Christianity is monotheistic, meaning it believes in one, only God.

Question: In what way is God holy?

Answer: The holiness of God means His absolute purity, perfection, and separation from all sin and evil.

Question: What is the love of God according to Christianity?

Answer: The love of God is described as unconditional, self-sacrificing, and salvific, best manifested in the sacrifice of Jesus Christ.

Question: How does Christianity understand the concept of God's justice?

Answer: God's justice means that God always acts in accordance with His own moral and legal principles, and that He will ultimately ensure justice in the universe.

Question: Is God involved in human affairs?

Answer: Yes, Christianity teaches about divine providence, meaning God is actively involved in human life and directs history towards His purposes.

Question: Can God be experienced directly?

Answer: Yes, many believers claim to have experienced God directly, though such experiences are subjective and vary from person to person.

Question: What does the doctrine of the Holy Trinity mean in Christianity?

Answer: The doctrine of the Holy Trinity signifies the belief in one God in three persons: the Father, the Son, and the Holy Spirit, who are coessential and coeternal.

Question: Where does the concept of the Holy Trinity come from?

Answer: The concept of the Holy Trinity originates from the Holy Scriptures and was developed by early Christian theologians to explain the biblical testimony about God.

Question: Is each person of the Trinity considered to be fully God?

Answer: Yes, each person of the Trinity is fully and equally God, yet there is only one God.

Question: What are the relationships between the persons of the Holy Trinity?

Answer: The persons of the Trinity live in eternal relationships of love and mutual self-giving, being a model of perfect unity.

Question: Is the word "Trinity" explicitly mentioned in the Bible?

Answer: The word "Trinity" does not appear in the Bible, but it is a theological term used to describe the biblical teaching about the three Divine persons.

Question: What are the biblical foundations for the doctrine of the Holy Trinity?

Answer: The biblical foundations for the doctrine of the Trinity include various passages where the three persons are mentioned, such as the baptism of Jesus or the baptismal formula in Matthew 28:19.

Question: What are the roles of the individual persons of the Trinity in the work of salvation?

Answer: The Father plans salvation, the Son accomplishes salvation through His incarnation, death, and resurrection, and the Holy Spirit applies the work of salvation in the lives of believers.

Question: Is the Holy Trinity common to all major Christian denominations?

Answer: Yes, the doctrine of the Trinity is common to Catholicism, Orthodoxy, and most Protestant branches.

Question: What are the differences in understanding the Holy Trinity among various Christian denominations?

Answer: The main differences concern the understanding of the relationships between the persons of the Trinity, especially regarding the procession of the Holy Spirit, which is a subject of dispute between the Catholic and Orthodox Churches.

Question: How does the Holy Trinity influence the life of a Christian?

Answer: The Holy Trinity is a model for the Christian

community, inspiring love, unity, and personal relationships, and is also the source of spiritual life and prayer.

Question: Are there any graphic symbols representing the Holy Trinity?

Answer: Yes, there are various symbols, such as the equilateral triangle or three interlocking circles, which attempt to represent the mystery of the Holy Trinity.

Question: Is prayer to one person of the Trinity also a prayer to the entire Trinity?

Answer: Yes, because all persons of the Trinity are inseparably united, prayer to one person is simultaneously a prayer to the entire Trinity.

Question: What are the challenges associated with understanding the doctrine of the Trinity?

Answer: The main challenge is the transcendent nature of the Trinity, which surpasses human understanding and logic, making it one of the most mysterious Christian doctrines.

Question: Does the Holy Trinity play a role in Christian sacraments?

Answer: Yes, the Holy Trinity is central in the sacraments, for example, in baptism, where a person is baptized "in the name of the Father, and of the Son, and of the Holy Spirit".

Question: What are the historical evidences for the existence of Jesus Christ?

Answer: Evidence for Jesus's existence comes from historical documents, including records by Roman and Jewish historians such as Tacitus and Josephus, as well as the New Testament and other early Christian writings.

Question: How is Jesus described in the Gospels?

Answer: The Gospels present Jesus as a teacher, healer, miracle worker, prophet, Messiah, and the Son of God, who came to save humanity.

Question: Why is Jesus called the Son of God?

Answer: Jesus is called the Son of God because Christianity teaches that He was conceived by the Holy Spirit and born of a virgin, indicating His divine origin and unique relationship with God the Father.

Question: What is the significance of Jesus's incarnation for Christians?

Answer: The incarnation, or God becoming human in the person of Jesus Christ, is crucial for Christians as it means God shared human experience, including suffering, enabling a direct relationship with God.

Question: What did Jesus teach about the Kingdom of God?

Answer: Jesus taught that the Kingdom of God is near, it is a spiritual reality where God's values like love, justice, and peace reign, and it is accessible to all who repent and believe in the Gospel.

Question: What are the main themes of Jesus's teachings?

Answer: The main themes of Jesus's teachings are love for God and neighbor, forgiveness of sins, humility, mercy, justice, and the necessity of conversion.

Question: What is the significance of Jesus's death on the cross?

Answer: Jesus's death on the cross is central in Christianity as it is seen as a sacrifice for the sins of humanity, opening the way for reconciliation with God and eternal life.

Question: What does Jesus's resurrection mean for Christians?

Answer: Jesus's resurrection is the foundation of the Christian faith, as it confirms His divinity, victory over death and sin, and gives hope for personal resurrection and eternal life.

Question: What are the differences in the portrayal of Jesus in the four Gospels?

Answer: Each of the Gospels highlights different aspects of Jesus's life and mission: Matthew presents Jesus as the Messiah fulfilling prophecies, Mark as the suffering Servant, Luke as the universal Savior, and John as the Incarnate Word and Son of God.

Question: Why did Jesus often speak in parables?

Answer: Jesus used parables to teach deep spiritual truths in an accessible way, often using familiar images and situations to the listeners.

Question: What miracles are attributed to Jesus and what is their significance?

Answer: Jesus is attributed with numerous miracles, including healings, raising the dead, and control over nature. These miracles are signs of His divine power and compassion and confirm His teachings.

Question: Did Jesus have siblings?

Answer: The Gospels mention brothers and sisters of Jesus, but there is theological debate whether they were

His biological siblings or cousins or close relatives.

Question: What is the significance of the "Our Father" prayer taught by Jesus?

Answer: The "Our Father" prayer is a model of Christian prayer, summarizing key elements of the relationship with God: worship, obedience to His will, request for daily needs, forgiveness, and deliverance from evil.

Question: Did Jesus claim to be God?

Answer: Jesus did not directly say "I am God", but many of His statements, especially in the Gospel of John, are interpreted by Christians as equivalent to a declaration of divinity, e.g., "I and the Father are one" (John 10:30).

Question: What does it mean that the Bible is "inspired" by God?

Answer: The assertion that the Bible is "inspired" means that Christians believe the biblical authors wrote under the influence of the Holy Spirit, making their writings a reliable account of God's revelation.

Question: What evidence is there that the Bible is inspired by God?

Answer: Evidence for the Bible's inspiration often includes its coherence despite many authors and a long period of composition, fulfillment of prophecies, and its enduring impact on people's lives and cultures.

Question: Are all parts of the Bible equally important and inspired?

Answer: While all biblical books are considered inspired, different Christian traditions may place varying emphasis on individual books or passages.

Question: How should Christians interpret difficult passages in the Bible?

Answer: Difficult passages in the Bible should be interpreted in the context of the entire biblical message, considering historical and cultural background, and in dialogue with the tradition and teaching of the Church.

Question: What is biblical hermeneutics?

Answer: Biblical hermeneutics is the science of interpreting biblical texts, helping to understand their meaning in the original context and their application in the contemporary world.

Question: What are the different methods of interpreting the Bible?

Answer: Methods of interpreting the Bible include literal, historical-critical, allegorical, typological, literary, and theological approaches, among others.

Question: Is the Bible infallible in all its statements?

Answer: Most Christians believe the Bible is infallible in matters of faith and morality, but there are varying views on its infallibility in historical and scientific matters.

Question: What are the arguments for the historicity and reliability of the Gospels?

Answer: Arguments for the historicity of the Gospels include early dating of their composition, consistency with external historical sources, and complex and detailed accounts that are difficult to invent.

Question: Are there apocryphal books that were not included in the Bible's canon?

Answer: Yes, there are apocryphal books that were not

included in the Bible's canon by various Christian communities for various reasons, including late dating, uncertain authorship, or content inconsistent with accepted doctrine.

Question: How do the Catholic and Protestant churches differ in terms of the canon of Scripture?

Answer: The main difference is that the Catholic Church accepts several deuterocanonical books (called apocrypha by Protestants) that are not recognized by most Protestant churches.

Question: What is exegesis?

Answer: Exegesis is the critical interpretation of biblical texts, aimed at extracting their original meaning and understanding their message.

Question: What role does tradition play in the interpretation of the Bible?

Answer: Tradition plays an important role in the interpretation of the Bible, providing historical and theological context that helps understand how the early Church understood and applied biblical teaching.

Question: Can the Bible be a source of teaching on contemporary social and moral issues?

Answer: Yes, many Christians believe the Bible provides principles and values that can be applied to considerations of contemporary social and moral issues.

Question: What are the main moral messages contained in the Bible?

Answer: The main moral messages of the Bible include love for God and neighbor, justice, mercy, peace, honesty, and responsibility for creation, among others.

Question: What criteria were used to determine the canon of Scripture?

Answer: Criteria for determining the canon included apostolic origin, widespread use in liturgy, consistency with the rule of faith, and testimony from the early Church.

Question: Why do different Christian denominations have different books in their Bibles?

Answer: Differences arise from historical decisions regarding the canon, which were made in various periods and contexts by different Christian communities.

Question: Is the Bible a sufficient source of faith, or is Tradition also needed?

Answer: Protestants typically teach "Sola Scriptura", meaning the Bible is a sufficient source of faith, while Catholics and Orthodox recognize both Scripture and Tradition as co-operating authorities.

Question: What are the main challenges in interpreting the Bible in the modern world?

Answer: Challenges include cultural and linguistic differences, scientific advancements that may question traditional understanding, and a variety of theological and philosophical perspectives.

Question: What role does archaeology play in understanding the biblical context?

Answer: Archaeology provides physical evidence that can confirm or explain historical accounts in the Bible and helps understand the cultural and historical background of the text.

Question: Do newly discovered biblical manuscripts

impact our understanding of the text?

Answer: Newly discovered manuscripts, such as the Dead Sea Scrolls, can provide new information about early versions of biblical texts and interpretative practices.

Question: What are the differences between Catholic and Protestant approaches to biblical interpretation?

Answer: Catholics typically emphasize the role of the Church's Magisterium as an interpretative authority, while Protestants more often emphasize individual study and interpretation of Scripture.

Question: Are there contemporary translations of the Bible that are more accurate than others?

Answer: There are various translations that strive to be as close to the original texts in the source languages, but each translation may have its strengths and weaknesses depending on the translation methodology used.

Question: What are the challenges associated with translating the Bible into modern languages?

Answer: Challenges include conveying nuances of the original languages, cultural differences, and avoiding the translator's doctrinal biases.

Question: Can the Bible be interpreted metaphorically, rather than literally?

Answer: Yes, many Christian traditions accept metaphorical or allegorical interpretations of the Bible, especially in relation to poetic and apocalyptic texts.

Question: What are the main principles of responsible Bible interpretation?

Answer: Principles of responsible interpretation include

respecting the historical and literary context of the text, avoiding eisegesis (imposing one's ideas onto the text), and seeking understanding in dialogue with the Church's tradition.

Question: Does the Bible say anything about its own authority?

Answer: Yes, for example, 2 Timothy 3:16 states that "All Scripture is God-breathed and is useful", which is often cited in reference to biblical authority.

Question: What are the differences in the interpretation of the Old Testament by Christians and Jews?

Answer: Christians often interpret the Old Testament through the lens of the New Testament and the life of Jesus, while Jewish interpretation focuses on the Old Testament as a standalone revelation.

Question: Can the Bible provide guidance on contemporary ethical dilemmas, such as genetic engineering or artificial intelligence?

Answer: Although the Bible does not directly address such modern issues, its moral and ethical principles can be applied as a framework for considering these dilemmas.

Question: What are the arguments for the Bible still being relevant in modern times?

Answer: Arguments for the Bible's relevance include its timeless moral and spiritual messages, its influence on shaping culture and society, and personal testimonies of people who experience its impact on their lives.

Question: Can guidance on financial management and business be found in the Bible?

Answer: Yes, the Bible provides principles on honesty, fair treatment of workers, avoiding greed, and responsible resource management.

Question: What are the differences between fundamentalist and liberal approaches to the Bible?

Answer: Fundamentalism typically emphasizes a literal interpretation of the Bible and adherence to traditional doctrines, while a liberal approach might accept more metaphorical interpretations and adapt biblical teachings to contemporary contexts.

Question: What are the consequences of rejecting the authority of the Bible?

Answer: Rejecting the authority of the Bible can lead to a variety of moral and spiritual interpretations, and in some cases, to secularization or the loss of a common reference point for faith and practice.

Question: Does the Bible contain contradictions? If so, how are they explained?

Answer: Some parts of the Bible may appear contradictory, but they are often explained through a deeper understanding of the cultural, literary, or historical context in which they were written.

Question: What are the principles for the proper use of biblical quotations?

Answer: Biblical quotes should be used in a way that respects their context and message, avoiding taking verses out of context or using them to justify biases.

Question: Can the Bible be a source of inspiration for non-believers?

Answer: Yes, even non-believers can draw ethical values,

life wisdom, and insight into the cultural foundations of Western civilization from the Bible.

Question: What are the methods of scientific study of the biblical text?

Answer: Methods of scientific study of the biblical text include textual, historical, form and source criticism, as well as literary and theological analysis.

Question: Does the Bible provide unequivocal answers to all moral questions?

Answer: The Bible provides general moral principles, but it does not always give clear-cut answers to specific, contemporary moral questions, requiring interpretation and application of these principles to particular situations.

Question: What is the importance of cultural context in interpreting the Bible?

Answer: Cultural context is crucial for understanding the Bible, as many of its books were written in different times and cultures, affecting their content and message.

Question: Can the Bible be used as a history textbook?

Answer: The Bible contains many historical accounts, but it is not a history textbook in the modern sense; it should be read considering its religious and moral purpose.

Question: What are the differences in approach to the Old Testament between Christianity and Judaism?

Answer: Christianity often interprets the Old Testament in the context of the New Testament and the messianic role of Jesus, while Judaism treats it as a complete divine revelation in itself.

Question: Does the Bible say anything about environmental protection?

Answer: The Bible includes principles for managing natural resources and caring for creation, which can be interpreted as guidelines for environmental protection.

Question: How can scientific discoveries be reconciled with the biblical account of creation?

Answer: Some Christians interpret the biblical account of creation metaphorically or allegorically, seeing in it deeper theological truths that are not necessarily contradictory to the scientific understanding of the universe.

Question: What is salvation in the context of Christianity?

Answer: Salvation in Christianity is the process through which people are saved from sin and its consequences through faith in Jesus Christ, leading to eternal life with God.

Question: What are the different Christian views on how to achieve salvation?

Answer: Different Christian denominations have varying views, but generally, they can be categorized as salvation through faith, grace, works, or a combination of these elements.

Question: Is there certainty of salvation, or is it a state that can be lost?

Answer: Some traditions, like Calvinism, teach the perseverance of the saints (once saved, always saved), while others, like Catholicism, recognize that the state of grace can be lost through mortal sin.

Question: How does Christianity define heaven?

Answer: Heaven is typically perceived as a place or state of being where saved souls are in eternal presence of God, experiencing full happiness and peace.

Question: Is hell a literal place of suffering, or a state of separation from God?

Answer: Interpretations of hell vary; some traditions treat it as a literal place of eternal suffering, while others view it as a metaphorical state of total separation from God.

Question: What is purgatory according to Catholic doctrine?

Answer: Purgatory, in Catholic doctrine, is a temporary state of purification for souls that died in a state of grace but still need purification from sins before entering heaven.

Question: Do all people have a chance at salvation, or only the elect?

Answer: Most Christian traditions teach that salvation is available to all through Christ, but they differ in views on predestination and free will.

Question: What are the different interpretations of the resurrection of the body?

Answer: Some traditions believe in the literal resurrection of the physical body, while others interpret resurrection as spiritual or symbolic.

Question: Can children who die before baptism be saved?

Answer: Many Christian traditions teach that God in His grace can save children who die before baptism, though the exact understanding of this issue varies among denominations.

Question: What are Christian views on reincarnation?

Answer: Traditional Christianity rejects the idea of reincarnation, teaching that people live once, and after death comes judgment and eternity.

Question: Are there biblical evidences for the existence of heaven and hell?

Answer: Yes, there are numerous references in the Bible, both in the Old and New Testaments, that speak of heaven and hell as eschatological realities.

Question: Do visions of heaven and hell in literature and art have biblical bases?

Answer: Many depictions of heaven and hell in culture are inspired by biblical descriptions, but they are often expanded or altered through artistic interpretation.

Question: What are the different Christian interpretations of the Apocalypse in the context of eschatology?

Answer: Interpretations of the Apocalypse range from viewing the prophecies as a literal description of future events to a symbolic understanding as a depiction of spiritual truths.

Question: Does Christianity believe in life after death, and if so, what is its nature?

Answer: Christianity teaches that there is life after death, which includes eternal existence in the presence of God (heaven) or separation from God (hell), depending on the state of the soul at death.

Question: Is there a possibility of conversion and salvation after death?

Answer: Most Christian traditions teach that decisions about faith and salvation are made during life, but some doctrines, like the doctrine of purgatory in Catholicism, allow for a kind of purification after death.

Question: What are the biblical foundations for beliefs about life after death?

Answer: Biblical foundations for beliefs about life after death are found in many passages, including Jesus' words about eternal life, descriptions of heaven in Revelation, and Paul's discussions about resurrection.

Question: Is there a difference between "those who sleep in Christ" and "the dead in sin"?

Answer: Yes, in the New Testament, "those who sleep in Christ" often refers to those who have died with faith in Christ and await resurrection, whereas "the dead in sin" may refer to those who died without faith.

Question: Are heaven and hell states of the soul or actual places?

Answer: This depends on the interpretation; some traditions view heaven and hell as actual places, while others see them as states of being of the soul after death.

Question: What actions or attitudes can jeopardize salvation according to Christian doctrine?

Answer: Mortal sins, rejecting faith, lack of repentance, and unforgiveness are examples of attitudes that can jeopardize salvation in Christian doctrine.

Question: Is there a concept of a "second chance" for salvation in Christianity?

Answer: Traditional Christianity teaches that life on earth is the only chance for accepting salvation, although some contemporary theologies consider the possibility of God's mercy after death.

Question: What are the different Christian views on the fate of the souls of infants and small children?

Answer: Views vary; some traditions, like Catholicism, taught about limbo for infants, but modern theologies often emphasize God's mercy and hope for the salvation of all innocents.

Question: Is there a relationship between behavior on earth and the state in the afterlife?

Answer: Yes, Christianity teaches that moral choices and behavior on earth have a direct impact on the state of the soul after death.

Question: Can visions of heaven and hell differ for each person?

Answer: Some theologies suggest that the experience of heaven and hell may be subjective and differ depending on the individual's relationship with God.

Question: What are Christian interpretations of the "eternal fire" mentioned in the Bible?

Answer: Interpretations of the "eternal fire" range from understanding it as a metaphor for separation from God to a literal interpretation as a place of punishment.

Question: Are there differences in the conception of heaven and hell among different Christian denominations?

Answer: Yes, there are significant differences, for example, some denominations do not believe in the existence of purgatory, and others have unique interpretations of resurrection.

Question: Are there religious practices that can aid in achieving salvation?

Answer: Yes, practices such as prayer, participation in sacraments, good deeds, and repentance are often seen as aiding the process of salvation.

Question: Is there a possibility of redemption for those who have committed serious sins?

Answer: Christianity teaches that repentance and God's mercy are available to all, even those who have committed serious sins, provided there is sincere conversion.

Question: What are the different Christian views on the final judgment?

Answer: Views on the final judgment vary; some traditions speak of an individual judgment immediately after death, while others taught about a universal resurrection and judgment in the future.

Question: Is there a concept of a "new heaven and new earth" in Christianity?

Answer: Yes, the concept of a "new heaven and new earth" appears in the Book of Revelation and refers to a future state where God creates a renewed world without sin and death.

Question: What are Christian views on the relationship between the soul and the body after death?

Answer: Most Christian traditions teach that the soul is immortal and continues to exist after the death of the body, and that there will be a future resurrection of the body and its reunification with the soul.

Question: Is there a possibility of changing the soul's location after death, for example, from hell to heaven?

Answer: Traditional Christianity teaches that the state of the soul after death is final and unchangeable, though some theologies open discussion on God's mercy after death.

Question: Are there different levels of reward in heaven or punishment in hell?

Answer: Some traditions, like Catholicism, speak of different degrees of glory in heaven, while others suggest that punishment in hell may vary depending on the severity of sins.

Question: What are Christian interpretations of the "book of life" mentioned in the Bible?

Answer: The "book of life" is often interpreted as a metaphorical record of those who are saved and have a share in eternal life.

Question: Is there a concept of "eternal rest" for souls in Christianity?

Answer: Yes, "eternal rest" is often used to describe the state of souls in heaven, where there is no longer suffering, sorrow, or pain.

Question: Does Christianity offer any explanation for the existence of evil and suffering in the context of life after death?

Answer: Christianity explains the existence of evil and suffering as a result of original sin and free will, but teaches that life after death is free from these realities.

Question: What are Christian views on visions of heaven and hell that some people claim to have experienced?

Answer: Opinions are divided; some traditions treat these

experiences as possible revelations or visions, while others approach them skeptically, advising caution in interpretation.

Question: Is there a concept of the "eternal city" in Christianity?

Answer: Yes, the "eternal city", often identified as the New Jerusalem, is described in Revelation as a place where God dwells among people, and eternal peace and justice reign.

Question: Does Christianity teach the possibility of the salvation of souls from hell?

Answer: Most Christian traditions teach that hell is a final state with no possibility of salvation, although some theological discussions on this topic continue.

Question: What are the different interpretations of God's light in the context of life after death?

Answer: God's light is often interpreted as a symbol of God's presence, love, and truth, which the souls in heaven experience.

Question: Is there a concept of "eternal life" in Christianity independent of heaven?

Answer: "Eternal life" in Christianity is usually synonymous with being in God's presence, i.e., heaven, but some interpretations may extend this concept beyond the traditional understanding.

Question: What are Christian views on the "second death" mentioned in Revelation?

Answer: The "second death" is often interpreted as the final separation from God, i.e., hell, for those who are separated from God after the final judgment.

Question: Is there a concept of "eternal judgment" in Christianity?

Answer: Yes, "eternal judgment" refers to the final judgment of God, where each soul is judged and receives eternal salvation or condemnation.

Question: What are the different forms of prayer in Christianity?

Answer: In Christianity, there are various forms of prayer, including adoration, supplication, thanksgiving, confession of sins, and asking for help for oneself and others.

Question: Can prayer change God's will?

Answer: Christianity teaches that prayer does not change God's immutable plan, but it can be a means through which God accomplishes His will in our lives.

Question: How often should we pray?

Answer: The New Testament encourages constant prayer, meaning maintaining continuous communication with God throughout the day.

Question: Does prayer have to be expressed in words?

Answer: Prayer does not have to be limited to words; it can also be expressed through thoughts, feelings, and even through silence and contemplation.

Question: What is the significance of group prayer compared to individual prayer?

Answer: Group prayer, such as in church or small groups, builds community and allows believers to support each other, while individual prayer is personal time with God.

Question: Are there specific body postures that are preferred during prayer?

Answer: While there is no one "correct" posture for prayer, some traditions prefer kneeling, standing, sitting, or raising hands as an expression of respect and humility.

Question: What is the significance of the "Our Father" prayer?

Answer: The "Our Father" is a prayer taught by Jesus, serving as a model for prayer, encompassing many key elements such as worship, petition, and forgiveness.

Question: Can prayer be a form of meditation?

Answer: Yes, prayer can be a form of meditation when we focus on God's word, His attributes, or His action in our lives, leading to deeper understanding and inner peace.

Question: What are the effects of constant prayer?

Answer: Constant prayer can lead to a deeper awareness of God's presence, greater resistance to temptations, and a more peaceful and purposeful life.

Question: Can prayer be informal, or does it always need to be structured?

Answer: Prayer can be both informal and structured; it is important that it is sincere and reflects a personal relationship with God.

Question: What are biblical examples of effective prayer?

Answer: The Bible contains many examples of effective prayer, including Hannah's prayer for a son, David's prayer for forgiveness, and Jesus' prayer in the Garden of Gethsemane.

Question: Can prayer aid in physical and emotional healing?

Answer: Many believe that prayer can contribute to healing, both physical and emotional, though not always in the way we expect.

Question: What is the role of prayer in dealing with life's difficulties?

Answer: Prayer can be a source of comfort, strength, and direction in difficult times, helping us find peace in God's presence and His promises.

Question: Can prayer influence the decisions of others?

Answer: Christianity teaches that prayer can impact situations and people's hearts, but always in harmony with free will and God's plan.

Question: What are Christian prayer practices during holiday seasons?

Answer: During holiday seasons, such as Advent or Lent, Christians often engage in special prayers and services that prepare their hearts for these special times.

Question: Can prayer be an act of worship without specific requests?

Answer: Yes, prayer can be a pure act of worship, focusing on praising God for His nature and works, without presenting specific requests.

Question: What is the significance of prayer before meals?

Answer: Prayer before meals is a form of thanking God for His goodness and provision, and a reminder of the spiritual aspect of daily life.

Question: Can prayer be spontaneous?

Answer: Yes, prayer can be spontaneous, expressing our immediate feelings, thoughts, and needs to God.

Question: What is the place of prayer in forgiveness and reconciliation?

Answer: Prayer is a key element in the process of forgiveness and reconciliation, helping us open our hearts to God's love and guidance in resolving conflicts.

Question: Can prayer be a tool for evangelization?

Answer: Prayer can prepare people's hearts to receive the Gospel and open doors for conversations about faith.

Question: What is the significance of prayer in life decisions?

Answer: Prayer in life decisions helps seek and recognize God's will and receive wisdom and direction.

Question: Can prayer be a form of spiritual warfare?

Answer: Yes, prayer is often seen as a weapon in spiritual warfare, protecting us from evil and strengthening our spiritual resilience.

Question: What is the significance of prayer in the context of inner healing?

Answer: Prayer can be a means of inner healing, helping us deal with emotional wounds and spiritual struggles.

Question: Can prayer assist in the development of virtues?

Answer: Prayer is fundamental in developing virtues, as through it we ask for God's grace and strength to practice good deeds.

Question: What are Christian methods for teaching children to pray?

Answer: Christian methods for teaching children to pray include personal example, simple and understandable prayers, and encouraging conversation with God in their own words.

Question: Can prayer be an act of social justice?

Answer: Prayer can inspire and motivate actions for social justice, asking for God's intervention and wisdom in action.

Question: What is the significance of prayer in the context of death and mourning?

Answer: In the context of death and mourning, prayer can be a source of comfort, hope in eternal life, and support in the grieving process.

Question: Is there a "best" time for prayer during the day?

Answer: While there is no one "best" time for prayer, many Christians find value in morning prayer to dedicate the day to God, and evening prayer for reflection and thanksgiving.

Question: What are biblical guidelines for praying for rulers and leaders?

Answer: The Bible encourages prayers for all in authority, so that we may live peaceful and godly lives, giving honor to God.

Question: Can prayer be replaced by other forms of spirituality?

Answer: Prayer is a unique element of Christian spirituality and cannot be completely replaced, although other spiritual practices can complement it.

Question: What is the significance of fasting in conjunction with prayer?

Answer: Fasting combined with prayer can deepen our focus on God, allowing for spiritual purification and strengthening our prayers.

Question: Can prayer be an act of sacrifice?

Answer: Yes, prayer can be a sacrifice of time and attention, expressing our love and devotion to God.

Question: What is the place of prayer in married life and family?

Answer: Prayer in marriage and family can strengthen bonds, build unity, and assist in the spiritual upbringing of children.

Question: Can prayer be a form of social action?

Answer: Prayer can inspire social action and be a support for those working for societal changes.

Question: What is the significance of prayer in the context of healing relationships?

Answer: Prayer can assist in healing relationships, asking for God's wisdom, love, and forgiveness between individuals.

Question: Can prayer be an act of obedience?

Answer: Prayer as an act of obedience reflects our willingness to listen and act according to God's will.

Question: What are the effects of a lack of prayer in Christian life?

Answer: A lack of prayer can lead to spiritual weakening, a loss of sense of God's presence, and less resilience to life's difficulties.

Question: Can prayer be an act of justice?

Answer: Prayer as an act of justice can be a request for God's intervention in unjust situations and help for the oppressed.

Question: What is the significance of prayer in the context of the sanctity of life?

Answer: Prayer in the context of the sanctity of life is an expression of respect for God's creation and a request for the protection of every life from conception to natural death.

Question: Can prayer be an act of worship outside of church?

Answer: Yes, prayer as an act of worship can be practiced in any place and time, reflecting our continuous relationship with God.

Question: What is the significance of prayer in the context of spiritual leadership?

Answer: Prayer is crucial for spiritual leadership, as it helps leaders to stay focused on God and His guidance in making decisions and guiding others.

Section 3: Questions on Religious Practices - Sexual Morality, Marriage, and Family

Question: What are the Christian principles regarding sexual morality?

Answer: Christianity teaches that sexuality should be expressed within the confines of marriage between a man and a woman, with respect and love.

Question: What is the sacrament of marriage in Christianity?

Answer: The sacrament of marriage is a sacred union between a man and a woman, seen as a reflection of the relationship between Christ and the Church.

Question: What are Christian guidelines for raising children?

Answer: Christianity emphasizes raising children in love, discipline, and religious teaching, focusing on their moral and spiritual development.

Question: What is the Christian stance on divorce?

Answer: While Christianity regards marriage as a lifelong commitment, some denominations accept divorce in certain circumstances, such as marital infidelity or domestic violence.

Question: How does Christianity approach the issue of contraception?

Answer: Attitudes towards contraception vary among denominations; some accept it as a means of family planning, while others advocate for abstinence and natural family planning methods.

Question: What are Christian principles regarding gender and gender identity?

Answer: Traditional Christianity typically aligns gender identity with biological sex, though modern discussions in this field are diverse and complex.

Question: What is the importance of love and fidelity in Christian marriage?

Answer: Love and fidelity are key elements of Christian marriage, reflecting the commitment and devotion between spouses and mirroring Christ's love for the Church.

Question: How does Christianity address marital and family issues?

Answer: Christianity encourages addressing marital and family issues through communication, prayer, counseling, and seeking God's wisdom.

Question: What is the Christian approach to adoption and foster care?

Answer: Adoption and foster care are viewed in Christianity as noble acts of love and caring for children in need of a family home.

Question: What are Christian principles regarding the professional work of both spouses?

Answer: Christianity teaches that decisions about professional work should be made with consideration of family welfare, mutual support, and balance between professional and family life.

Question: What is the importance of forgiveness and reconciliation in marriage?

Answer: Forgiveness and reconciliation are crucial in

Christian marriage, enabling the healing of relationships and growth in love and understanding.

Question: How does Christianity approach the issue of childlessness in marriage?

Answer: Christianity treats childlessness as a challenge that can be an opportunity for spiritual growth and exploring other forms of parenthood, such as adoption.

Question: What is the role of prayer and spirituality in family life?

Answer: Prayer and spirituality are fundamental in family life, helping to build strong, healthy, and spiritually oriented relationships.

Question: What are Christian principles for raising children in faith?

Answer: Raising children in faith involves biblical teaching, personal example, participation in church life, and encouraging a personal relationship with God.

Question: How does Christianity view premarital relationships?

Answer: Traditionally, Christianity teaches that sexual relations should be confined within marriage, promoting abstinence before marriage.

Question: Does Christianity accept interfaith marriages?

Answer: Attitudes towards interfaith marriages vary among denominations; some accept them under certain conditions, while others recommend marrying within the same faith.

Question: What are Christian principles regarding the

roles of men and women in marriage?

Answer: Christianity traditionally teaches about different but complementary roles for men and women in marriage, though contemporary interpretations can vary among denominations.

Question: How does Christianity address the issue of domestic violence?

Answer: Christianity condemns all forms of domestic violence, encouraging seeking safety, support, and appropriate counseling.

Question: What is the Christian approach to the role of sexuality in marriage?

Answer: In Christianity, sexuality within marriage is viewed as a gift from God, meant to express love, intimacy, and cooperation in procreation.

Question: What are Christian principles regarding the adoption of children by same-sex couples?

Answer: Attitudes towards adoption by same-sex couples vary among denominations; some are opposed, while others accept such adoptions as an act of love and care.

Question: How does Christianity approach the issues of divorce and remarriage?

Answer: Many Christian denominations allow divorce and remarriage in certain situations, though they advise caution and seeking spiritual counsel.

Question: What is the importance of spiritual leadership in the family?

Answer: Spiritual leadership in the family includes leading by example, prayer, teaching, and supporting family members in their spiritual growth.

Question: How does Christianity address the challenges of modern parenting?

Answer: Christianity encourages parents to seek wisdom in the Scriptures, church community, and spiritual counseling in dealing with the challenges of modern parenting.

Question: What are Christian principles regarding the role of parents in the sexual education of children?

Answer: Christianity teaches that parents should be the primary educators in matters of sexuality, conveying values based on biblical principles of morality and love.

Question: What is the role of prayer in resolving family conflicts?

Answer: Prayer can be an important tool in resolving family conflicts, helping in the search for God's wisdom, reconciliation, and love.

Question: What are Christian principles regarding the care of elderly family members?

Answer: Christianity teaches respect and care for older family members, recognizing their dignity and worth.

Question: What is the importance of family participation in church life?

Answer: Family participation in church life strengthens family bonds, supports spiritual growth, and builds a community of faith.

Question: How does Christianity approach issues of sexual orientation and gender identity?

Answer: Christianity has varying approaches to sexual orientation and gender identity, from traditional views to more open interpretations, depending on the denomination and theological beliefs.

Question: How does Christianity interpret celibacy and its place in spiritual life?

Answer: Celibacy is often seen in Christianity as a gift and a calling to fully dedicate oneself to God's service, especially among clergy and consecrated persons.

Question: What are Christian principles regarding homosexual relationships?

Answer: Attitudes towards homosexual relationships vary among denominations; some adhere to traditional teachings of marriage as a union between a man and a woman, while others accept and bless same-sex unions.

Question: What is the Christian approach to fertility and infertility treatment?

Answer: Christianity generally supports seeking infertility treatment, provided it is consistent with biblical principles of respect for life and marriage.

Question: What are Christian principles regarding the role of sex in marriage?

Answer: Sex in Christian marriage is seen as an expression of love, intimacy, and cooperation in procreation, in line with God's plan for marriage.

Question: How does Christianity deal with the issue of marital infidelity?

Answer: Christianity condemns marital infidelity as a serious violation of marital vows, encouraging reconciliation and forgiveness in the context of repentance and healing.

Question: What is the Christian approach to parents' role in religious education of children?

Answer: Christianity teaches that parents play a key role in the religious education of children, passing on the faith through teaching, example, and participation in church life.

Question: What are Christian principles regarding family planning?

Answer: Christianity promotes responsible family planning, in accordance with moral principles and respect for life; attitudes towards contraceptive methods vary among denominations.

Question: What is the importance of love and respect in raising children?

Answer: Love and respect are the foundation of Christian child-rearing, helping children develop a healthy sense of self-worth and spiritual understanding.

Question: How does Christianity approach the issues of divorce and remarriage?

Answer: Christianity approaches divorce and remarriage cautiously, encouraging seeking spiritual counsel and understanding of God's plan for marriage.

Question: What is the role of prayer in marriage and family?

Answer: Prayer is seen as a key element in marriage and family, strengthening spiritual bonds and aiding in everyday challenges.

Question: How does Christianity deal with challenges

associated with modern technologies in the family context?

Answer: Christianity encourages mindful and responsible use of modern technologies, with an emphasis on protecting family and spiritual values.

Question: What are Christian principles regarding parents' role in shaping the moral attitudes of children?

Answer: Christianity teaches that parents play a key role in shaping the moral attitudes of children, setting an example and teaching principles based on the Bible.

Question: What is the importance of family participation in church activities?

Answer: Family participation in church activities is important for spiritual growth, building community, and passing on the faith.

Question: What are Christian principles regarding parents' role in dealing with children's behavioral problems?

Answer: Christianity encourages parents to approach children's behavioral problems with love, patience, and understanding, seeking wisdom in prayer and biblical principles, and utilizing professional support when necessary.

Question: How does Christianity approach the issues of poverty and social inequality?

Answer: Christianity teaches the necessity of helping the poor and working for social justice, emphasizing love for one's neighbor and sharing resources.

Question: What is the Christian stance on immigration

and refugees?

Answer: Christianity encourages hospitality and compassion towards immigrants and refugees, seeing them as an opportunity to demonstrate neighborly love and service.

Question: How does Christianity address environmental protection and climate change?

Answer: Christianity recognizes the responsibility for caring for creation and encourages actions to protect the environment and combat climate change as part of ethical responsibility.

Question: What is the Christian approach to economics and economic justice?

Answer: Christianity promotes economic justice, fair business practices, and care for the poor, emphasizing a balance between profit and ethical responsibility.

Question: How does Christianity address issues of racism and discrimination?

Answer: Christianity condemns racism and discrimination, teaching the equality of all people before God and the necessity of building a just society.

Question: What is the Christian stance on war and peace?

Answer: Christianity generally promotes peace and reconciliation, though different denominations have varying approaches to issues of war and national defense.

Question: How does Christianity deal with corruption and dishonesty in politics?

Answer: Christianity teaches honesty, transparency, and

accountability in public life, condemning corruption as inconsistent with Christian values.

Question: What is the Christian approach to human rights and civil liberties?

Answer: Christianity supports the respect for human rights and civil liberties, recognizing the dignity of every person created in the image of God.

Question: How does Christianity address gender equality and women's rights?

Answer: Christianity has varying approaches to gender equality; some denominations actively support women's rights and equality, while others adhere to more traditional gender roles.

Question: What is the Christian stance on education and science?

Answer: Christianity generally supports education and science as means to better understand the world and God, though there are differing views on specific issues such as the theory of evolution.

Question: How does Christianity approach public health and healthcare?

Answer: Christianity emphasizes the importance of healthcare and caring for the body as a temple of the Holy Spirit, advocating for access to healthcare for all.

Question: What is the Christian approach to technology and social media?

Answer: Christianity encourages responsible use of technology and social media, emphasizing the need to uphold moral and ethical values in the digital world.

Question: How does Christianity address addiction and mental health issues?

Answer: Christianity highlights the importance of supporting and caring for individuals struggling with addiction and mental health problems, promoting spiritual healing and renewal.

Question: What is the Christian stance on globalization and its impact on society?

Answer: Christianity examines globalization in terms of its impact on social justice, poverty, and inequality, encouraging actions that support just and sustainable development.

Question: How does Christianity address the rights of people with disabilities?

Answer: Christianity teaches the dignity and worth of every individual, calling for equal rights and opportunities for people with disabilities.

Question: What is the Christian approach to the issue of homelessness?

Answer: Christianity encourages active involvement in assisting the homeless, seeing it as an expression of neighborly love and concern for those in need.

Question: How does Christianity deal with challenges related to migration and integration?

Answer: Christianity promotes a compassionate and just approach to migrants, emphasizing the importance of integration and mutual respect.

Question: What is the Christian stance on human trafficking and modern-day slavery?

Answer: Christianity strongly condemns human trafficking and all forms of slavery as fundamental violations of human dignity.

Question: How does Christianity address economic equality and tax justice?

Answer: Christianity encourages the construction of a just economic system that supports equality and justice, including fair tax practices.

Question: What is the Christian approach to violence in media and culture?

Answer: Christianity promotes a culture of peace and respect, critically assessing the impact of violence in media on society.

Question: How does Christianity deal with challenges related to new technologies and ethics?

Answer: Christianity encourages an ethical approach to new technologies, emphasizing their impact on human dignity and society.

Question: What is the Christian stance on bioethics and genetic engineering?

Answer: Christianity approaches bioethics and genetic engineering cautiously, highlighting the need to protect human dignity and ethical boundaries in science.

Question: How does Christianity address the issue of an aging society and care for seniors?

Answer: Christianity teaches respect and care for the elderly, emphasizing their value and the need for dignified care.

Question: What is the Christian approach to

sustainable development?

Answer: Christianity promotes sustainable development as a way of caring for creation and future generations, encouraging responsible resource management.

Question: How does Christianity address animal rights and environmental ethics?

Answer: Christianity recognizes the importance of caring for creation, including animals, emphasizing humane treatment and environmental protection.

Question: What is the Christian stance on cybersecurity and online privacy?

Answer: Christianity underscores the importance of protecting privacy and security in the digital world, encouraging ethical use of technology.

Question: How does Christianity deal with challenges related to global humanitarian crises?

Answer: Christianity calls for active involvement in humanitarian aid and support for victims of crises, emphasizing neighborly love and solidarity.

Question: What is the Christian approach to sexual education and reproductive health?

Answer: Christianity has diverse approaches to sexual education and reproductive health, often emphasizing the importance of morality and ethics in these matters.

Question: How does Christianity relate to the issues of national security and defense?

Answer: Christianity emphasizes the pursuit of peace and justice but also recognizes the right to national defense, with varying approaches depending on denominations.

Question: What is the Christian stance on the issues of drugs and the legalization of psychoactive substances?

Answer: Christianity generally condemns the abuse of psychoactive substances, emphasizing the need to protect public health and societal well-being.

Question: How does Christianity address challenges related to unemployment and poverty?

Answer: Christianity calls for active efforts to combat poverty and unemployment, promoting social justice and assistance to those in need.

Question: What is the Christian approach to domestic violence and the protection of victims?

Answer: Christianity condemns all forms of domestic violence and calls for the protection of victims, offering support and help in regaining dignity.

Question: How does Christianity deal with the issue of discrimination based on sexual orientation or gender identity?

Answer: Christianity has various approaches to this issue, ranging from full acceptance and support to more conservative positions, always emphasizing the dignity of every person.

Question: What is the Christian stance on freedom of speech and censorship?

Answer: Christianity supports freedom of speech as a value but also emphasizes the need for responsibility and respect in communication.

Question: How does Christianity address challenges related to climate migration?

Answer: Christianity calls for solidarity and support for those affected by climate change, emphasizing the need for global responsibility and cooperation.

Question: What is the Christian approach to sustainable transportation and urbanization?

Answer: Christianity promotes sustainable development and responsible resource management, including in the areas of transportation and urbanization.

Question: How does Christianity deal with the issue of technology addiction and digital media?

Answer: Christianity encourages moderate and mindful use of technology, emphasizing the importance of balance between digital life and the real world.

Question: What is the Christian stance on food safety and GMOs?

Answer: Christianity underscores the importance of protecting health and the environment, taking various positions on GMOs and food safety.

Question: How does Christianity address challenges related to global inequalities?

Answer: Christianity calls for action to reduce global inequalities, promoting justice and equality.

Question: What is the Christian approach to data protection and privacy?

Answer: Christianity emphasizes the importance of protecting personal data and privacy as elements of human dignity and digital ethics.

Question: How does Christianity deal with the issue of gambling addiction and games of chance?

Answer: Christianity condemns gambling addiction as harmful and destructive, promoting a healthy and responsible approach to finances.

Question: What is the Christian stance on educational equality and access to education?

Answer: Christianity supports equal access to education as a key element of social justice and personal development.

Question: What are the origins of Christianity?

Answer: Christianity traces its origins to the teachings of Jesus Christ in the 1st century AD in Judea and quickly spread throughout the Roman Empire.

Question: What were the main reasons for the spread of Christianity in the early centuries?

Answer: The spread of Christianity resulted from apostolic missions, the universal appeal of its message, and the extensive network of roads and communication in the Roman Empire.

Question: What was the significance of the Council of Nicaea for the development of Christianity?

Answer: The Council of Nicaea in 325 AD was crucial in unifying Christian doctrine, especially regarding the nature of Christ and the Holy Trinity.

Question: What were the main causes and effects of the East-West Schism in 1054?

Answer: The East-West Schism led to the division of Christianity into the Eastern (Orthodox) and Western (Catholic) Churches, differing doctrinally and liturgically.

Question: What were the causes and consequences of the Reformation in the 16th century?

Answer: The Reformation, initiated by Martin Luther, was a response to abuses in the Catholic Church and resulted in the emergence of Protestantism and further divisions within Christianity.

Question: What was the significance of the Counter-Reformation for the Catholic Church?

Answer: The Counter-Reformation was the Catholic Church's response to the Reformation, leading to internal reforms, redefinition of doctrines, and increased missionary activity.

Question: What were the major missionary movements in the history of Christianity?

Answer: Missionary movements included early apostolic missions, the expansion of Christianity in the Middle Ages, colonial missions, and contemporary global evangelization efforts.

Question: What were the consequences of the Reformation for the development of the modern world?

Answer: The Reformation contributed to the development of modern nation-states, religious pluralism, and had an impact on culture, science, and politics.

Question: What was the significance of renewal movements in the 20th century for Christianity?

Answer: Renewal movements, such as Pentecostalism, revitalized Christianity by emphasizing personal faith experiences and the work of the Holy Spirit.

Question: What were the major ecumenical events in the 20th century?

Answer: Important ecumenical events included the establishment of the World Council of Churches and various initiatives for dialogue among different Christian denominations.

Question: What were the influences of Christianity on

the development of Western civilization?

Answer: Christianity had a significant influence on the development of Western philosophy, art, law, science, and ethical systems.

Question: What were the main controversies and heresies in the history of Christianity?

Answer: Throughout the history of Christianity, there were numerous controversies and heresies, such as Arianism, Pelagianism, and Gnosticism, which influenced the development of doctrine.

Question: What was the significance of the Crusades for Christianity?

Answer: The Crusades had a significant impact on the relationship between Christianity and Islam, European politics, and the territorial expansion of Christianity.

Question: What were the effects of geographical discoveries on the spread of Christianity?

Answer: Geographical discoveries facilitated the spread of Christianity to new continents, often accompanied by colonization and cultural changes.

Question: What were the main consequences of the English Reformation for Christianity?

Answer: The English Reformation led to the establishment of the Anglican Church, the separation from Rome, and changes in liturgy and doctrine in England.

Question: What was the significance of the Council of Trent for the Catholic Church?

Answer: The Council of Trent was a pivotal moment in the Counter-Reformation, redefining Catholic doctrine and introducing reforms in the education of clergy and liturgy.

Question: What were the influences of Christianity on the development of education and universities?

Answer: Christianity had a significant impact on the development of the education system, including the creation of the first universities in Europe.

Question: What were the major renewal movements in the Catholic Church in the 20th century?

Answer: In the 20th century, the Catholic Church experienced renewal movements, such as the Second Vatican Council, which introduced significant changes in liturgy and the Church's approach to the world.

Question: What were the effects of the development of the printing press on the spread of Christianity?

Answer: The invention of the printing press enabled the wider distribution of the Bible and Christian literature, which played a crucial role in the Reformation and religious education.

Question: What were the major events in the history of the Eastern Orthodox Church?

Answer: Important events in the history of the Eastern Orthodox Church include the East-West Schism, the development of monasticism, and its influence on Eastern European culture.

Question: What was the significance of charismatic movements in Christianity?

Answer: Charismatic movements, emphasizing the work of the Holy Spirit and charismatic gifts, had a significant impact on the renewal and dynamism of many Christian communities.

Question: What were the consequences of the Great Western Schism for the Catholic Church?

Answer: The Great Western Schism, characterized by rival popes, weakened the authority of the papacy and contributed to later reforms.

Question: What were the influences of Christianity on the development of art and architecture?

Answer: Christianity had a profound influence on the development of art and architecture, from early Christian art to the Renaissance and Baroque periods.

Question: What were the main theological controversies in the Eastern Orthodox Church?

Answer: The Eastern Orthodox Church experienced theological controversies, such as iconoclasm and disputes over hesychasm, which influenced its spiritual and doctrinal development.

Question: What were the effects of the Enlightenment on Christianity?

Answer: The Enlightenment posed challenges to Christianity, including religious criticism and the promotion of rationalism, but also inspired reflection and dialogue.

Question: What was the significance of ecumenical movements for Christianity?

Answer: Ecumenical movements aimed to promote unity among different Christian denominations, contributing to dialogue and cooperation.

Question: What were the major events in the history of Protestantism?

Answer: In the history of Protestantism, significant events included various reform movements, the development of denominations, and their impact on society and culture.

Question: What was the importance of Christian missions in the colonial era?

Answer: Christian missions in the colonial era had a significant influence on the spread of Christianity as well as on local cultures and communities.

Question: What were the main causes and consequences of radical Reformation?

Answer: The radical Reformation, represented by Anabaptists and other groups, emphasized the need for personal conversion and adult baptism, leading to conflicts with the mainstream Reformation movements and Catholicism.

Question: What was the significance of the First Vatican Council for the Catholic Church?

Answer: The First Vatican Council, convened in the 19th century, defined the dogma of papal infallibility and contributed to the consolidation of Catholic doctrine.

Question: What were the influences of Christianity on the development of law and legal systems?

Answer: Christianity had a significant influence on the development of law, including shaping moral and ethical principles in legislation.

Question: What were the major renewal movements in Protestantism?

Answer: In Protestantism, important renewal movements included the evangelical awakening, which emphasized personal faith and involvement in church life.

Question: What were the effects of the Reformation on the development of democracy and religious freedom?

Answer: The Reformation contributed to the development of ideas about freedom of conscience and belief, influencing the later development of democracy and religious pluralism.

Question: What were the major events in the history of the Catholic Church in the 20th century?

Answer: In the 20th century, the Catholic Church experienced significant events, such as the Second Vatican Council, the development of liberation theology, and responses to contemporary social challenges.

Question: What was the importance of monastic movements for Christianity?

Answer: Monastic movements played a crucial role in preserving and developing spiritual life, education, and culture in the Middle Ages.

Question: What were the influences of Christianity on the development of literature and poetry?

Answer: Christianity had a significant impact on the development of literature and poetry, inspiring many writers and poets from the Middle Ages to the present day.

Question: What were the major theological controversies in the Catholic Church?

Answer: The Catholic Church has experienced numerous theological controversies, such as debates over the nature of Christ, predestination, and the role of Mary.

Question: What were the effects of scientific discoveries on Christianity?

Answer: Scientific discoveries, especially during the Enlightenment and modern period, posed challenges to Christian cosmology and anthropology but also inspired theological reflection.

Question: What were the major events in the history of the Eastern Orthodox Church in the 20th century?

Answer: In the 20th century, the Eastern Orthodox Church grappled with political challenges like communism and issues related to ecumenism and modernization.

Question: What was the significance of Protestant movements in North America?

Answer: Protestant movements in North America had a significant impact on shaping society, culture, and politics, particularly in the United States.

Question: What were the effects of the Industrial Revolution on Christianity?

Answer: The Industrial Revolution brought challenges to Christianity, such as urbanization, poverty, and ethical issues related to labor and capitalism.

Question: What was the importance of feminist movements for Christianity?

Answer: Feminist movements influenced Christianity by sparking discussions about the role of women in the church, feminist theology, and gender equality.

Question: What are the main doctrinal differences between Catholicism and Protestantism?

Answer: The main differences concern the authority of the Pope, the role of Tradition, sacraments, justification by faith, and the interpretation of the Bible.

Question: How does the Eastern Orthodox Church differ from the Catholic Church?

Answer: Differences include church structure, liturgy, certain theological aspects like the filioque controversy, and the role of the Patriarch of Constantinople.

Question: What are the distinctive characteristics of Anglicanism?

Answer: Anglicanism combines elements of Catholicism and Protestantism, with a unique church structure, liturgy, and theological approach.

Question: What are the major branches of Protestantism and their characteristics?

Answer: Major branches include Lutheranism, Calvinism, Anglicanism, Methodism, and Baptism, each with differences in doctrine, liturgy, and church organization.

Question: What are the specific features of the Eastern Orthodox Church?

Answer: The Eastern Orthodox Church emphasizes tradition, mysticism, iconography, and liturgy.

Question: How do Evangelical Churches differ from other Protestant denominations?

Answer: Evangelical Churches emphasize justification by faith, the authority of Scripture, and personal relationship with God.

Question: What are the main characteristics of Methodism?

Answer: Methodism emphasizes holiness of life, systematic Bible study, and social activism.

Question: What are the distinctive elements of Baptism?

Answer: Baptism stands out with its practice of adult baptism by immersion, emphasis on the autonomy of local congregations, and evangelistic efforts.

Question: What are the specific features of the Seventh-day Adventist Church?

Answer: Seventh-day Adventists observe the Sabbath on Saturday, await the second coming of Christ, and emphasize a healthy lifestyle.

Question: What are the main differences between the Catholic Church and the Eastern Orthodox Church?

Answer: Differences include the authority of the Pope, the filioque clause in the Creed, liturgy, and certain practices and traditions.

Question: How does the Lutheran Church differ from other Protestant denominations?

Answer: Lutheranism emphasizes justification by faith, the central teachings of Martin Luther, and a specific form of liturgy.

Question: What are the characteristic features of Calvinism?

Answer: Calvinism emphasizes God's sovereignty, predestination, and a strong work ethic.

Question: What are the specific features of the Pentecostal Church?

Answer: Pentecostalism stands out with its emphasis on the work of the Holy Spirit, speaking in tongues, healing, and dynamic worship.

Question: What are the main characteristics of the Russian Orthodox Church?

Answer: The Russian Orthodox Church has strong ties to the state, a rich liturgical and monastic tradition, and a unique history and culture.

Question: What are the main differences between the Catholic Church and the Anglican Church?

Answer: The differences concern the authority of the Pope, some aspects of the sacraments, and the role of Tradition and Scripture in doctrine.

Question: How does the Greek Orthodox Church differ from other Orthodox Churches?

Answer: The Greek Orthodox Church has a unique history, culture, and liturgical traditions, although it shares most doctrines with other Orthodox Churches.

Question: What are the characteristic features of the Presbyterian Church?

Answer: Presbyterianism is characterized by a church government structure based on elders, Calvinist theology, and active engagement in social issues.

Question: What are the main branches of the Orthodox Church?

Answer: Major branches include the Russian Orthodox Church, Greek Orthodox Church, Serbian Orthodox Church, and others, each with cultural and historical distinctions.

Question: How do Baptist Churches differ from other Protestant denominations?

Answer: Baptist Churches emphasize adult baptism by

immersion, the autonomy of local congregations, and evangelism.

Question: What are the specific features of the Methodist Church?

Answer: Methodism stands out with its emphasis on holiness of life, systematic Bible study, and active social involvement.

Question: What are the characteristic elements of the Seventh-day Adventist Church?

Answer: Seventh-day Adventists observe the Sabbath on Saturday, await the second coming of Christ, and emphasize a healthy lifestyle.

Question: What are the main differences between the Catholic Church and the Eastern Orthodox Church?

Answer: Differences concern the authority of the Pope, the filioque clause in the Creed, liturgy, and certain practices and saintly traditions.

Question: How does the Lutheran Church differ from other Protestant denominations?

Answer: Lutheranism emphasizes justification by faith, the central teachings of Martin Luther, and a specific form of liturgy.

Question: What are the distinctive characteristics of the Calvinist Church?

Answer: Calvinism is characterized by a strong emphasis on God's sovereignty, predestination, and a strong work ethic.

Question: What are the specific features of the Pentecostal Church?

Answer: Pentecostalism stands out with its emphasis on the work of the Holy Spirit, speaking in tongues, healing, and dynamic worship.

Question: What are the main characteristics of the Russian Orthodox Church?

Answer: The Russian Orthodox Church has strong ties to the state, a rich liturgical and monastic tradition, and a unique history and culture.

Question: What are the main differences between the Catholic Church and the Anglican Church?

Answer: The differences concern the authority of the Pope, some aspects of the sacraments, and the role of Tradition and Scripture in doctrine.

Question: How does the Greek Orthodox Church differ from other Orthodox Churches?

Answer: The Greek Orthodox Church has a unique history, culture, and liturgical traditions, although it shares most doctrines with other Orthodox Churches.

Question: What are the main characteristics of the Episcopal Church in the United States?

Answer: American Anglicanism, known as Episcopalism, is characterized by theological diversity, a strong emphasis on liturgy, and an active role in social issues.

Question: How does the Orthodox Church in America differ from traditional Orthodox Churches in Europe?

Answer: Orthodoxy in America combines various ethnic traditions, is more open to ecumenical dialogue, and adapts to the American cultural context.

Question: What are the distinctive features of the

Lutheran Church in Scandinavia?

Answer: Scandinavian Lutheranism is closely tied to national traditions, characterized by liberal theology, and actively engaged in social issues.

Question: What are the main branches of the Baptist Church?

Answer: Baptist branches include the Southern Baptist Convention, Independent Baptists, and other groups with theological and practice differences.

Question: How does the Methodist Church in the United Kingdom differ from Methodism in the USA?

Answer: British Methodism has strong historical roots, is more conservative in theology and practices than American Methodism.

Question: What are the specific characteristics of the Seventh-day Adventist Church in Latin America?

Answer: Adventists in Latin America emphasize evangelism, education, health, with strong community and cultural ties.

Question: What are the main differences between the Catholic Church and Eastern Churches?

Answer: Eastern Churches differ from Catholicism in liturgy, sacramental theology, and some aspects of doctrine, though they are in full communion.

Question: How does the Calvinist Church in the Netherlands differ from other Calvinist branches?

Answer: Dutch Calvinism has strong historical roots, characterized by theological conservatism and active engagement in social life.

Question: What are the characteristic features of the Pentecostal Church in Brazil?

Answer: Brazilian Pentecostalism is dynamic, with a strong emphasis on healing and miracles, and an active role in impoverished communities.

Question: What are the main characteristics of the Coptic Orthodox Church in Egypt?

Answer: Egyptian Orthodoxy, mainly the Copts, has an ancient tradition, unique liturgy, and a strong sense of cultural identity.

Question: How does the Anglican Church in Africa differ from Anglicanism in other parts of the world?

Answer: Anglicanism in Africa blends traditional liturgical elements with local cultures, often taking a more conservative theological approach.

Question: What are the specific characteristics of the Lutheran Church in Germany?

Answer: German Lutheranism is closely tied to the history of the Reformation, characterized by theological diversity, and actively involved in ecumenical dialogue.

Question: What are the main branches of the Baptist Church in Africa?

Answer: African Baptist branches differ in theology and practices, often combining traditional Christianity with local cultures.

Question: How does the Methodist Church in Africa differ from Methodism in other parts of the world?

Answer: African Methodism combines traditional Methodism with local cultures and issues, often focusing on social justice and development.

Question: How does Christianity relate to Judaism in the context of its roots?

Answer: Christianity originated from Judaism and shares many common beliefs but differs in matters of messianism and the interpretation of the Scriptures.

Question: How do Christianity and Islam perceive each other?

Answer: Both religions recognize themselves as monotheistic and have some common biblical figures, but they differ in doctrinal and theological matters.

Question: What are the main differences between Christianity and Buddhism?

Answer: Although both religions promote ethics of love and compassion, they differ significantly in theological aspects, such as the concept of God and salvation.

Question: How does Christianity adapt to different cultures around the world?

Answer: Christianity adapts through inculturation, integrating its teachings with local traditions and customs while preserving key doctrinal elements.

Question: How does interreligious dialogue impact Christianity?

Answer: Interreligious dialogue helps in understanding and respecting other beliefs, as well as seeking common values and solutions to global issues.

Question: How does Christianity relate to Hinduism?

Answer: Christianity and Hinduism differ significantly in

theological matters but can find common ground in teachings of love, compassion, and spirituality.

Question: What challenges do Christians face in Muslim-majority countries?

Answer: Christians in Muslim-majority countries may encounter challenges related to religious freedom, discrimination, and the need for interreligious dialogue.

Question: What are the similarities and differences between Christianity and Confucianism?

Answer: While differing in theological matters, both traditions emphasize ethics, family harmony, and social responsibility.

Question: How does Christianity influence intercultural relations?

Answer: Christianity can serve as a bridge between cultures, promoting understanding, tolerance, and cooperation among different communities.

Question: How does Christianity relate to new religious movements?

Answer: Christianity often analyzes new religious movements for compatibility with its teachings while maintaining openness to dialogue and understanding.

Question: What are the challenges for Christianity in the context of globalization?

Answer: Globalization poses challenges for Christianity related to religious pluralism, maintaining identity, and adapting to a rapidly changing world.

Question: How can Christianity contribute to interreligious peace?

Answer: Christianity can promote interreligious peace through dialogue, cooperation in conflict resolution, and joint actions for social justice.

Question: What are the main challenges in Christian-Jewish dialogue?

Answer: Challenges include overcoming historical prejudices, theological differences, and jointly seeking understanding and respect.

Question: How can Christianity contribute to understanding and accepting cultural diversity?

Answer: By promoting values such as love for one's neighbor, respect for the dignity of each person, and active engagement in intercultural dialogue.

Question: How does Christianity interpret the phenomenon of religious syncretism?

Answer: Christianity often approaches syncretism cautiously, aiming to maintain doctrinal purity while understanding the need for cultural adaptation.

Question: How can Christianity contribute to intercultural development?

Answer: Through education, dialogue, and cooperation, Christianity can promote mutual understanding and respect among different cultures.

Question: What are the challenges in the dialogue between Christianity and Eastern religions?

Answer: The main challenges include differences in the perception of God, salvation, spiritual practices, as well as the need for mutual respect and understanding.

Question: How does Christianity relate to indigenous

religions and beliefs?

Answer: Christianity seeks to build bridges of understanding and respect while preserving its key doctrines and values.

Question: How can Christianity contribute to global interreligious dialogue?

Answer: By actively participating in dialogue, education, and joint initiatives, Christianity can promote peace and understanding among different religions.

Question: What are the challenges for Christianity in the context of growing religious pluralism?

Answer: Challenges include maintaining religious identity, openness to dialogue, and adaptation to a diverse environment.

Question: How can Christianity contribute to resolving interreligious conflicts?

Answer: By promoting principles of forgiveness, reconciliation, and cooperation, Christianity can play a crucial role in conflict resolution.

Question: What are the main differences between Christianity and Sikhism?

Answer: The main differences concern the perception of God, religious practices, and the role of sacred scriptures in both religions.

Question: How can Christianity contribute to understanding and accepting sexual diversity?

Answer: By promoting love, respect, and the dignity of every person, Christianity can contribute to building a more inclusive and accepting community.

Question: How does Christianity relate to new spiritual and esoteric movements?

Answer: Christianity often analyzes these movements for compatibility with its own teachings while remaining open to dialogue and understanding.

Question: How can Christianity contribute to environmental protection in the context of different cultures?

Answer: By promoting the ethics of stewardship and collaborating with various cultures, Christianity can play a crucial role in environmental conservation.

Question: What are the challenges for Christianity in the context of growing materialism and consumerism?

Answer: Challenges include promoting spiritual and ethical values in the face of a dominant materialistic culture.

Question: How can Christianity contribute to social and economic development in different cultures?

Answer: Through charitable, educational, and social activities, Christianity can support the development and improvement of living conditions in various communities.

Question: How does Christianity address the challenges related to migration and cultural integration?

Answer: Christianity promotes principles of hospitality, respect for diversity, and support for the social integration of migrants.

Question: How does Christianity address the challenges of globalization and social changes?

Answer: Christianity seeks to respond to these challenges through adaptation, intercultural dialogue, and the promotion of universal ethical values.

Question: How can Christianity contribute to understanding and accepting ethnic diversity?

Answer: By teaching the equality and dignity of all people, Christianity promotes respect and acceptance of ethnic diversity.

Question: What are the challenges for Christianity in the context of growing secularization?

Answer: Challenges include maintaining faith and religious practices in an increasingly secular world and finding ways to engage with modern society.

Question: How can Christianity contribute to interreligious dialogue in the context of conflicts?

Answer: By promoting principles of forgiveness, reconciliation, and cooperation, Christianity can play a key role in mitigating interreligious conflicts.

Question: How does Christianity address the challenges of new technologies and media?

Answer: Christianity seeks to use new technologies to spread its message while maintaining a critical approach to their impact on values and interpersonal relationships.

Question: How can Christianity contribute to sustainable development?

Answer: By promoting the ethics of stewardship and social justice, Christianity can support sustainable development and environmental protection.

Question: What are the challenges for Christianity in

the context of growing nationalism and populism?

Answer: Challenges include promoting universal Christian values such as love of neighbor and hospitality in the face of rising nationalist and populist tendencies.

Question: How can Christianity contribute to the promotion of peace and social justice?

Answer: Through active participation in peace efforts, social justice initiatives, and human rights advocacy, Christianity can play a crucial role in building a better world.

Question: How does Christianity address the challenges of gender and sexual orientation diversity?

Answer: Christianity seeks to find a balance between adhering to its doctrines and promoting respect and acceptance for all individuals, regardless of their gender or sexual orientation.

Question: How can Christianity contribute to the development of intercultural education?

Answer: By promoting education that respects cultural and religious diversity, Christianity can contribute to building a more open and understanding world.

Question: What are the challenges for Christianity in the context of growing religious diversity?

Answer: Challenges include maintaining Christian identity while being open to dialogue and cooperation with other religions.

Question: How can Christianity contribute to international cooperation?

Answer: By promoting principles of love, compassion, and

justice, Christianity can play a key role in international cooperation and addressing global issues.

Question: How does Christianity address the challenges of migration and refugees?

Answer: Christianity promotes principles of hospitality and care for refugees while seeking solutions that respect the dignity and rights of all individuals.

Question: How can Christianity contribute to understanding and accepting cultural diversity in education?

Answer: By integrating values such as tolerance, respect, and understanding of cultural diversity into educational programs, Christianity can contribute to the education of a more open and understanding society.

Section 5: Spiritual and Personal Questions - Developing Spiritual Life and Personal Relationship with God

Question: How can I begin building a personal relationship with God?

Answer: Initiating a personal relationship with God often starts with prayer, reading the Holy Scriptures, and reflecting on one's own life in the context of Christian teachings.

Question: How can I deepen my prayer life?

Answer: Deepening one's prayer life can be achieved through regular practice, meditation, participating in the life of the church community, and seeking personal spiritual experiences.

Question: What practices can help in the development of spiritual life?

Answer: Practices such as daily prayer, meditation, fasting, attending worship services, and studying the Bible are essential for the development of spiritual life.

Question: How can I experience the presence of God in my life?

Answer: Experiencing the presence of God is often connected to personal prayer, reflection, participation in sacraments, and awareness of God's action in everyday life.

Question: What are ways to overcome spiritual dryness?

Answer: Overcoming spiritual dryness requires patience,

regular prayer, seeking spiritual support, and being open to the grace of God.

Question: How can I better understand God's will in my life?

Answer: Understanding God's will requires prayer for discernment, studying the Holy Scriptures, seeking spiritual guidance, and listening to one's conscience.

Question: How can I deepen my knowledge of God?

Answer: Deepening one's knowledge of God can be achieved through studying theology, spiritual reading, participating in Bible study groups, and listening to sermons.

Question: What are ways to maintain consistency in spiritual life?

Answer: Maintaining consistency in spiritual life requires regular prayer, participation in church life, self-discipline, and a constant desire for spiritual growth.

Question: How can I integrate my faith into everyday life?

Answer: Integrating faith into everyday life involves consciously applying Christian principles in daily decisions, relationships, and actions.

Question: How can I develop spiritual resilience in the face of difficulties?

Answer: Developing spiritual resilience requires trust in God, accepting difficulties as part of spiritual life, and seeking support within the faith community.

Question: How can I better understand and interpret spiritual experiences?

Answer: Better understanding of spiritual experiences can be achieved through prayer for discernment, studying church teachings, and sharing one's experiences with fellow believers.

Question: How can I find a balance between spiritual and material life?

Answer: Finding balance involves recognizing the value of spiritual life, practicing moderation in material pursuits, and integrating Christian values into all aspects of life.

Question: How can I nurture a stronger connection with the Church as a faith community?

Answer: Nurturing a stronger connection with the Church requires active participation in parish life, involvement in church activities, and building relationships with fellow members of the community.

Question: How can I transform my daily actions into acts of prayer and sacrifice?

Answer: Transforming daily actions into acts of prayer and sacrifice involves dedicating these actions to God consciously and performing them with the intention of serving others.

Question: How can I recognize and respond to God's calling in my life?

Answer: Recognizing God's calling requires prayer, introspection, seeking spiritual guidance, and being open to the leading of the Holy Spirit.

Question: How can I overcome doubts in my faith?

Answer: Overcoming doubts often requires prayer, studying the Holy Scriptures, having conversations with clergy and fellow believers, and patiently seeking answers.

Question: How can I develop patience and humility in my spiritual life?

Answer: Developing patience and humility requires regular spiritual practice, reflection on one's own weaknesses, and trust in God's plan.

Question: How can I better cope with difficulties and suffering?

Answer: Coping with difficulties and suffering requires deep faith, the support of the faith community, prayer, and trust that God is present even in difficult moments.

Question: How can I develop gratitude as a part of my spiritual life?

Answer: Developing gratitude can be achieved through daily practices of thanksgiving, reflection on blessings, and recognizing God's presence in life.

Question: How can I better understand and practice forgiveness?

Answer: Better understanding and practicing forgiveness require studying Jesus' teachings, praying for the grace of forgiveness, and practicing forgiveness in daily relationships.

Question: How can I develop inner peace and spiritual harmony?

Answer: Developing inner peace and spiritual harmony requires regular prayer, meditation, avoiding conflicts, and focusing on God's presence.

Question: How can I find purpose and direction in my spiritual life?

Answer: Finding purpose and direction requires prayer for

discernment, reflection on one's talents and passions, and seeking ways to serve others.

Question: How can I develop humility and avoid spiritual pride?

Answer: Developing humility requires self-awareness, accepting one's limitations, regular prayer, and avoiding comparisons with others.

Question: How can I better resist temptations and sins?

Answer: Resisting temptations and sins requires prayer for strength, regular participation in sacraments, sincere confession, and avoiding occasions of sin.

Question: How can I develop spiritual resilience in the face of faith crises?

Answer: Developing spiritual resilience in the face of faith crises requires patience, seeking spiritual support, studying the Holy Scriptures, and being open to new perspectives.

Question: How can I deepen my relationship with Jesus Christ?

Answer: Deepening your relationship with Jesus Christ can be achieved through prayer, meditation on His life and teachings, and emulating His example in daily life.

Question: How can I develop spiritual sensitivity and empathy?

Answer: Developing spiritual sensitivity and empathy requires openness to the needs of others, regular prayer for mercy, and practicing active compassion.

Question: How can I find a balance between spiritual

life and secular responsibilities?

Answer: Finding balance requires planning, setting priorities, praying for wisdom, and consciously integrating spiritual values into daily life.

Question: How can I develop trust in God in the face of uncertainty and change?

Answer: Developing trust in God in the face of uncertainty requires prayer, reflection on God's promises in the Bible, and practicing faith even in difficult circumstances.

Question: How can I better recognize and respond to the work of the Holy Spirit in my life?

Answer: Better recognizing the work of the Holy Spirit requires prayer for discernment, openness to His guidance, and attentiveness to inner convictions and impulses.

Question: How can I cultivate joy and hope as elements of my spiritual life?

Answer: Cultivating joy and hope requires focusing on God's promises, practicing gratitude, and finding joy in everyday experiences.

Question: How can I develop a greater awareness of God's presence in my life?

Answer: Developing a greater awareness of God's presence requires regular prayer, meditation, and practicing mindfulness of God's actions in everyday situations.

Question: How can I better understand and practice neighborly love in my spiritual life?

Answer: Better understanding and practicing neighborly love require studying Jesus' teachings, empathy, and actively engaging in service to others.

Question: How can I develop a deeper sensitivity to the needs of others?

Answer: Developing a deeper sensitivity to the needs of others requires empathy, active listening, and involvement in charitable activities or volunteering.

Question: How can I find inspiration for spiritual growth in everyday life?

Answer: Finding inspiration for spiritual growth in everyday life requires seeking God's signs in daily experiences, spiritual reading, and conversations with fellow believers.

Question: How can I better cope with spiritual crises?

Answer: Coping with spiritual crises requires prayer, seeking spiritual support, patience, and openness to changing perspectives.

Question: How can I develop spiritual wisdom and understanding?

Answer: Developing spiritual wisdom and understanding requires studying the Holy Scriptures, reflecting on life experiences, and seeking spiritual guidance.

Question: How can I better integrate my spiritual life with family and work life?

Answer: Better integration of spiritual life with family and work life requires setting priorities, consciously sharing your faith with others, and seeking harmony between different aspects of life.

Question: How can I develop Christian virtues in my life?

Answer: Developing Christian virtues requires studying the examples of saints, practicing self-discipline, and actively striving to live according to evangelical values.

Question: How can I better understand and live by the principles of the Gospel?

Answer: Better understanding and living by the principles of the Gospel require regular reading of the Holy Scriptures, reflecting on Jesus' teachings, and applying these principles in daily life.

Question: How can I develop spiritual courage and strength in the face of adversity?

Answer: Developing spiritual courage and strength requires trust in God, seeking support in the faith community, and practicing resilience in difficult situations.

Question: How can I better understand and celebrate the sacraments as part of my spiritual life?

Answer: Better understanding and celebrating the sacraments require studying their significance, active participation in liturgy, and reflection on their role in spiritual life.

Question: How can I deal with doubts about the existence of God?

Answer: Dealing with doubts requires prayer, studying philosophical and theological arguments for the existence of God, and conversations with experienced clergy.

Question: What should I do when my prayers seem to be ineffective?

Answer: In such situations, it is important to maintain a regular prayer practice, seek spiritual support, and be patient while waiting for God's response.

Question: How can I regain faith after a traumatic event?

Answer: Regaining faith after a traumatic event may require time, support from the faith community, professional psychological help, and deep personal reflection.

Question: How can I reconcile scientific discoveries with my faith?

Answer: Reconciling science with faith requires understanding that science and religion can complement each other and studying theological interpretations of scientific discoveries.

Question: How can I deal with internal conflicts regarding my religious beliefs?

Answer: Dealing with internal conflicts requires openness to dialogue, seeking spiritual guidance, and accepting that doubts are a part of spiritual growth.

Question: What should I do when I feel distant from God?

Answer: In such situations, it is important to maintain a regular prayer practice, seek spiritual support, and be patient while waiting for a renewed relationship with God.

Question: How can I find answers to challenging theological questions?

Answer: Finding answers to challenging theological questions requires studying theology, participating in discussions, and seeking advice from experienced theologians.

Question: How can I cope with guilt and shame related to my past?

Answer: Coping with guilt and shame requires prayer for forgiveness, participation in the sacrament of reconciliation, and accepting God's mercy.

Question: How can I maintain faith in the face of suffering and injustice in the world?

Answer: Maintaining faith in the face of suffering requires deep reflection on the mystery of suffering, prayer for peace and justice, and engagement in actions for change.

Question: What should I do when my religious beliefs clash with the beliefs of my family or friends?

Answer: In such situations, it is important to seek dialogue, show respect for other beliefs, and maintain your own religious identity.

Question: How can I find meaning and purpose in my spiritual life?

Answer: Finding meaning and purpose requires deep reflection on your own life, prayer for discernment, and seeking ways to serve others.

Question: How can I overcome the fear of death and uncertainty about life after death?

Answer: Overcoming the fear of death requires reflection on Christian teachings about life after death, prayer for inner peace, and conversations with clergy.

Question: How can I cope with disappointment related to the Church or its members?

Answer: Coping with disappointment requires understanding that the Church consists of imperfect people and seeking support in healthy faith communities.

Question: How can I find a balance between faith and daily responsibilities?

Answer: Finding balance requires setting priorities, integrating spiritual practices into daily life, and seeking support in the faith community.

Question: How can I find inner peace in the face of internal conflicts and doubts?

Answer: Finding inner peace requires regular prayer, meditation, seeking spiritual support, and accepting that doubts are a natural part of spiritual growth.

Question: How can I reconcile different interpretations of the Bible that seem contradictory?

Answer: Reconciling different interpretations of the Bible requires studying the historical and cultural context of Scripture, seeking advice from experienced theologians, and being open to theological diversity.

Question: How can I maintain faith in the face of personal tragedies and losses?

Answer: Maintaining faith in the face of tragedy requires prayer, support from the faith community, professional psychological help, and time for mourning and healing.

Question: What should I do when I feel discouraged by the lack of answers to my prayers?

Answer: In such situations, it's important to maintain faith that God hears every prayer, seek spiritual support, and be patient while waiting for God's action.

Question: How can I cope with a sense of isolation in my faith?

Answer: Coping with a sense of isolation requires seeking a faith community, getting involved in church activities, and sharing your experiences with others.

Question: How can I find answers to questions about evil and suffering in the world?

Answer: Finding answers to questions about evil and suffering requires studying theological and philosophical perspectives on the problem of evil, praying for understanding, and engaging in actions for good.

Question: How can I find meaning in suffering and difficulties?

Answer: Finding meaning in suffering requires reflection on the Christian understanding of suffering, seeking personal growth through difficulties, and praying for strength and perseverance.

Question: What should I do when my religious beliefs are questioned or attacked?

Answer: In such situations, it's important to remain calm, seek wise and respectful dialogue, and strengthen your knowledge and beliefs.

Question: How can I cope with disappointment related to unfulfilled religious expectations?

Answer: Coping with disappointment requires a realistic view of expectations, praying for inner peace, and seeking new ways to experience faith.

Question: How can I find a balance between tradition and modernity in my faith?

Answer: Finding balance requires understanding the core principles of faith, being open to new perspectives, and seeking harmony between tradition and contemporary values.

Question: How can I cope with internal conflicts between faith and personal desires?

Answer: Coping with internal conflicts requires deep reflection on your own values, praying for discernment, and seeking balance between spirituality and everyday life.

Question: How can I find my way back to faith after a period of doubt?

Answer: Finding your way back to faith after a period of doubt requires patience, seeking spiritual support, participating in the life of the faith community, and being open to God's action.

Question: How can I cope with a sense of inadequacy in my spiritual life?

Answer: Coping with a sense of inadequacy requires accepting your limitations, seeking spiritual growth, and praying for humility and gratitude.

Question: How can I find answers to questions about the future of my faith and role in the Church?

Answer: Finding answers to questions about the future of your faith requires praying for discernment, getting involved in church activities, and seeking advice from experienced clergy.

Question: How can I find my way to a deeper faith after a period of religious indifference?

Answer: Finding the path to deeper faith after a period of indifference requires reengaging in spiritual practices, seeking inspiration in the teachings of the Church, and drawing from personal experiences with God.

Question: How can I deal with internal conflicts regarding my religious beliefs?

Answer: Dealing with internal conflicts requires openness to spiritual dialogue, seeking advice from experienced clergy, and accepting that faith can evolve.

Question: How can I find meaning and purpose in the suffering I experience?

Answer: Finding meaning and purpose in suffering requires reflecting on the Christian understanding of suffering as a path to spiritual growth, praying for strength, and seeking support from the faith community.

Question: What should I do when my religious beliefs seem to conflict with my professional or social environment?

Answer: In such situations, it's important to find a balance between staying true to your beliefs and respecting diversity in your environment.

Question: How can I cope with a sense of isolation caused by my faith?

Answer: Coping with a sense of isolation requires seeking a community that shares similar values and developing the ability to build bridges between different worldviews.

Question: How can I reconcile with past sins and mistakes?

Answer: Reconciliation with the past requires participation in the sacrament of reconciliation, accepting God's forgiveness, and working on personal growth and change.

Question: How can I find my way to faith in the face of skepticism and criticism?

Answer: Finding the path to faith in the face of skepticism requires openness to seeking truth, studying arguments for faith, and engaging in conversations with people who have deep spiritual lives.

Question: What should I do when I feel discouraged by the lack of understanding of my faith by others?

Answer: In such situations, it's important to maintain your religious identity, seek support among those with similar beliefs, and be patient in the face of misunderstanding.

Question: How can I cope with a sense of powerlessness in my spiritual life?

Answer: Coping with a sense of powerlessness requires praying for strength and wisdom, seeking spiritual support, and accepting that everyone goes through challenging moments in their faith.

Question: How can I find the path to a deeper understanding of my faith?

Answer: Finding the path to a deeper understanding of faith requires engaging in the study of Scripture, participating in spiritual formation, and having conversations with experienced clergy.

Question: How can I find a balance between spiritual life and daily responsibilities?

Answer: Finding balance requires setting priorities, integrating spiritual practices into daily life, and seeking support within the faith community.

Question: How can I deal with internal doubts about my faith?

Answer: Dealing with doubts requires openness to

spiritual exploration, conversations with clergy and experienced believers, and accepting that doubts are part of the process of spiritual growth.

Question: How can I find the path to deepening my relationship with God?

Answer: Deepening your relationship with God requires regular prayer, meditation, participation in the life of the faith community, and personal commitment to spiritual practices.

Question: How can I find answers to difficult questions about my faith?

Answer: Finding answers to difficult questions requires studying the teachings of the Church, seeking wise advice, and being open to spiritual exploration.

Question: How does Christianity explain the presence of suffering in the world?

Answer: Christianity sees suffering as a part of the human experience in a fallen world but also as an opportunity for spiritual growth and drawing closer to God.

Question: Does suffering have any value in Christian life?

Answer: Yes, suffering can be a means to deeper understanding of faith, growth in virtues like patience and compassion, and as a way to identify with the suffering of Christ.

Question: How can I find comfort in God during suffering?

Answer: Finding comfort in God during suffering can be achieved through prayer, meditation, studying the Scriptures, and receiving support from the faith community.

Question: What are Christian ways of dealing with life's difficulties?

Answer: Christian ways of dealing with difficulties include prayer, trusting in God's providence, seeking support within the faith community, and practicing patience and perseverance.

Question: Does God send suffering as punishment?

Answer: Christianity teaches that God is merciful and loving; suffering is usually not seen as a direct punishment from God but rather as a consequence of human free will and the brokenness of the world.

Question: How can I understand God's plan in the face of personal suffering?

Answer: Understanding God's plan in the face of suffering requires faith, prayer for wisdom and discernment, and trust that God can transform even difficult situations for good.

Question: Can suffering be a path to holiness?

Answer: Yes, in Christianity, suffering is often seen as a means to deeper union with Christ and a path to holiness through offering one's sufferings to God.

Question: How can I offer my suffering to God?

Answer: Offering your suffering to God requires a conscious act of will, prayer in which you surrender your difficulties to God, and seeking ways for your experiences to be of service to others.

Question: What are biblical examples of coping with suffering?

Answer: Biblical examples include figures like Job, who maintained faith in the face of suffering, and Paul, who experienced hardships but continued to preach the Gospel.

Question: Can prayer reduce my suffering?

Answer: Yes, prayer can be a source of comfort, strength, and inner peace, helping to alleviate the experience of suffering through spiritual support and a sense of God's presence.

Question: How can I help others in their suffering?

Answer: Helping others in their suffering involves offering emotional and spiritual support, prayer, practical assistance, and being present and compassionate.

Question: Can suffering lead to a deeper understanding of God's love?

Answer: Yes, suffering can lead to a deeper understanding of God's love as it allows one to experience His comfort, strength, and presence in challenging times.

Question: How can I maintain faith in the face of unexplained suffering?

Answer: Maintaining faith in the face of unexplained suffering requires trusting in God's wisdom, seeking support within the faith community, and accepting that not all aspects of suffering may be comprehensible.

Question: Are there Christian practices that can help transform suffering?

Answer: Yes, Christian practices such as meditation, contemplation, participation in the sacraments, and offering suffering can help transform suffering into a path of spiritual growth.

Question: How does Christianity explain the presence of suffering in the world?

Answer: Christianity sees suffering as a part of the human experience in a fallen world but also as an opportunity for spiritual growth and drawing closer to God.

Question: Does suffering have any value in Christian life?

Answer: Yes, suffering can be a means to deeper understanding of faith, growth in virtues like patience and compassion, and as a way to identify with the suffering of Christ.

Question: How can I find comfort in God during suffering?

Answer: Finding comfort in God during suffering can be achieved through prayer, meditation, studying the Scriptures, and receiving support from the faith community.

Question: What are Christian ways of dealing with life's difficulties?

Answer: Christian ways of dealing with difficulties include prayer, trusting in God's providence, seeking support within the faith community, and practicing patience and perseverance.

Question: Does God send suffering as punishment?

Answer: Christianity teaches that God is merciful and loving; suffering is usually not seen as a direct punishment from God but rather as a consequence of human free will and the brokenness of the world.

Question: How can I understand God's plan in the face of personal suffering?

Answer: Understanding God's plan in the face of suffering requires faith, prayer for wisdom and discernment, and trust that God can transform even difficult situations for good.

Question: Can suffering be a path to holiness?

Answer: Yes, in Christianity, suffering is often seen as a means to deeper union with Christ and a path to holiness through offering one's sufferings to God.

Question: How can I offer my suffering to God?

Answer: Offering your suffering to God requires a conscious act of will, prayer in which you surrender your difficulties to God, and seeking ways for your experiences to be of service to others.

Question: What are biblical examples of coping with suffering?

Answer: Biblical examples include figures like Job, who maintained faith in the face of suffering, and Paul, who experienced hardships but continued to preach the Gospel.

Question: Can prayer reduce my suffering?

Answer: Yes, prayer can be a source of comfort, strength, and inner peace, helping to alleviate the experience of suffering through spiritual support and a sense of God's presence.

Question: How can I help others in their suffering?

Answer: Helping others in their suffering involves offering emotional and spiritual support, prayer, practical assistance, and being present and compassionate.

Question: Can suffering lead to a deeper

understanding of God's love?

Answer: Yes, suffering can lead to a deeper understanding of God's love as it allows one to experience His comfort, strength, and presence in challenging times.

Question: How can I maintain faith in the face of unexplained suffering?

Answer: Maintaining faith in the face of unexplained suffering requires trusting in God's wisdom, seeking support within the faith community, and accepting that not all aspects of suffering may be comprehensible.

Question: Are there Christian practices that can help transform suffering?

Answer: Yes, Christian practices such as meditation, contemplation, participation in the sacraments, and offering suffering can help transform suffering into a path of spiritual growth.

Question: How does Christianity perceive suffering in the context of salvation?

Answer: Christianity sees suffering as an opportunity to share in the sufferings of Christ, which can lead to a deeper understanding of salvation and grace.

Question: Is there a way to see God's presence in suffering?

Answer: Yes, you can perceive God's presence in suffering through experiencing His comfort, strength, and guidance, especially in the most challenging moments.

Question: What are Christian perspectives on the suffering of the innocent?

Answer: Christianity recognizes the suffering of the

innocent as a profound moral and spiritual problem, emphasizing the need for compassion, justice, and trust that God will ultimately bring justice.

Question: How can I find inner peace in the face of suffering?

Answer: Inner peace in the face of suffering can be found through deep prayer, meditation, trusting in God's promise of His presence and support, and through the support of the faith community.

Question: Can suffering be an opportunity for a deeper understanding of neighborly love?

Answer: Yes, suffering can be an opportunity to develop compassion, empathy, and neighborly love, teaching us how to support others in their difficulties.

Question: What are Christian practices that can help transform suffering into hope?

Answer: Practices such as participating in the sacraments, prayer, studying the Scriptures, sharing your experiences with others, and actively seeking God's presence can help transform suffering into hope.

Question: Can suffering be a path to a deeper understanding of God's mercy?

Answer: Yes, suffering can lead to a deeper understanding of God's mercy as it allows you to experience His comfort and care, especially in the most challenging moments.

Question: How can I use my suffering as a testimony of faith?

Answer: You can use your suffering as a testimony of faith by sharing how God has worked in your life through difficult times and how your faith has been strengthened.

Question: Can suffering be a means to experience God's grace?

Answer: Yes, in suffering, we often experience God's grace in a more intense way because we become more aware of His support, love, and power.

Question: How can I maintain faith when suffering seems endless?

Answer: Maintaining faith in the face of prolonged suffering requires deep trust in God's goodness, regular prayer, support from the faith community, and focusing on God's eternal promises.

Question: Are there biblical figures that can serve as examples in coping with suffering?

Answer: Yes, figures like Job, David in the Psalms, and above all, Jesus Christ, are examples of endurance and trust in God in the midst of suffering.

Question: How can I find purpose in suffering that seems senseless?

Answer: Finding purpose in senseless suffering requires a spiritual understanding that God can transform even the most challenging situations for good and that our sufferings may have a deeper meaning in God's plan.

Question: Can suffering be an opportunity for a deeper understanding and experience of the church community?

Answer: Yes, suffering can be an opportunity for a deeper experience of the church community, as sharing your difficulties can lead to greater mutual support and assistance.

Question: How can I use my experiences of suffering

to deepen my understanding and service to others?

Answer: You can use your experiences of suffering to deepen your understanding and service to others through empathy, sharing your testimony, offering support and prayer, and actively participating in church and social activities.

Question: What role does the Church play in the life of an individual Christian?

Answer: The Church serves as a spiritual community that supports the development of faith, offers sacraments and teachings, and allows for the sharing of faith experiences with others.

Question: Why is participation in church life important for Christians?

Answer: Participation in church life is important because it strengthens faith through community, teaching, sacraments, and service, helping believers grow spiritually.

Question: What are the benefits of regular attendance at worship services?

Answer: Regular attendance at worship services strengthens faith, builds community, allows for collective worship of God, and provides spiritual nourishment through sermons and sacraments.

Question: How does the Church assist in personal spiritual growth?

Answer: The Church assists in personal spiritual growth through biblical teaching, spiritual support, administering sacraments, and providing opportunities for service to others.

Question: What is the significance of being part of a local church community?

Answer: Being part of a local church community provides a sense of belonging, mutual support, opportunities for service, and learning from fellow believers.

Question: Is church attendance essential to being a good Christian?

Answer: While personal faith is crucial, church attendance is recommended because it offers spiritual support, community, and sacraments that are important in Christian life.

Question: How does the Church support families and marriages?

Answer: The Church supports families and marriages through sacraments like marriage, formational programs, counseling, and activities aimed at building strong family relationships.

Question: What are ways to get involved in church life?

Answer: Ways to get involved include attending worship services, joining Bible study groups, volunteering, engaging in charitable activities, and participating in other church-related activities.

Question: How does the Church help in overcoming life's difficulties?

Answer: The Church offers spiritual support, prayer, counseling, and community, which can help individuals overcome life's difficulties.

Question: Can the Church assist in finding one's vocation in life?

Answer: Yes, the Church can help in discovering and nurturing one's vocation through spiritual guidance, teaching, and service opportunities.

Question: What is the significance of sacraments in a Christian's life?

Answer: Sacraments are visible signs of God's grace and play a crucial role in the spiritual life, strengthening faith and connecting believers with Christ.

Question: How does the Church aid in understanding and interpreting the Bible?

Answer: The Church helps in interpreting the Bible through sermons, Bible studies, teaching, and spiritual guidance, providing a deeper understanding of Scripture.

Question: What is the place of prayer in church life?

Answer: Prayer is a central element of church life, serving as a means of communication with God, expressing worship, seeking assistance, and giving thanks.

Question: Does the Church offer support in moral and ethical matters?

Answer: Yes, the Church provides support in moral and ethical matters through teaching, counseling, and spiritual guidance, assisting believers in making decisions in line with Christian values.

Question: What are the different roles of clergy and laity in the Church?

Answer: Clergy typically serve roles related to teaching, leading worship, and administering sacraments, while laity can engage in charitable, educational, organizational, and evangelistic activities within the Church.

Question: Is participation in parish life essential for Christian life?

Answer: Participation in parish life is recommended because it supports spiritual growth, builds community, and allows for active involvement in the life of the Church.

Question: What are the benefits of regular attendance at worship services?

Answer: Regular attendance at worship services strengthens faith, offers spiritual support, enables communal prayer and sacraments, and fosters a sense of community.

Question: How can the Church assist in personal spiritual development?

Answer: The Church offers teaching, sacraments, community, service opportunities, and spiritual support, all of which are essential for personal spiritual development.

Question: What is the significance of church holidays and liturgical seasons?

Answer: Church holidays and liturgical seasons help believers experience key moments of faith, teach and remind them of important events and Christian truths.

Question: Is involvement in church activities important for every Christian?

Answer: Yes, involvement in church activities is important because it allows for the practical expression of faith, community building, and serving others.

Question: What are different forms of service in the Church?

Answer: Different forms of service in the Church include charitable work, teaching, music ministry, pastoral care, prayer ministry, event organization, and many others.

Question: How does the Church support families and marriages?

Answer: The Church supports families and marriages through sacraments, counseling, support groups, education, and various programs designed for families.

Question: How does the Church contribute to the development of local communities?

Answer: The Church contributes to the development of local communities through charitable work, education, social support, community-building initiatives, and interfaith dialogue.

Question: What is the significance of missions and evangelism in the life of the Church?

Answer: Missions and evangelism are crucial for the life of the Church because they are a means of sharing the good news of Christ and expanding the kingdom of God.

Question: Should the Church engage in social and political issues?

Answer: Yes, the Church often engages in social and political issues to promote justice, peace, and the protection of human dignity, in accordance with its teachings and values.

Question: What are the challenges faced by the contemporary Church in the context of globalization?

Answer: Contemporary challenges for the Church include intercultural dialogue, adapting to a changing world, safeguarding human rights and the environment, and responding to secularization.

Question: What is the importance of ecumenism and interfaith dialogue for the Church?

Answer: Ecumenism and interfaith dialogue are important for the Church because they promote understanding, peace, and unity among different faith traditions.

Question: How can the Church contribute to the development of young people?

Answer: The Church can contribute to the development of young people through youth programs, education, spiritual support, service opportunities, and providing safe spaces for growth and exploration of faith.

Question: What are the biblical foundations for the role of the Church in the life of a Christian?

Answer: The biblical foundations for the role of the Church include Jesus' teachings on community, examples of the early Christian communities in the Acts of the Apostles, and the letters of Paul, which emphasize the importance of the Church as the Body of Christ.

Question: How can the Church help in overcoming personal crises of faith?

Answer: The Church can offer spiritual support, counseling, prayer, community, and teaching to help individuals overcome crises of faith.

Question: How does the Church contribute to promoting social justice?

Answer: The Church promotes social justice through teaching, charitable work, engagement in public affairs, and the defense of human rights.

Question: What is the significance of small groups and communities in the life of the Church?

Answer: Small groups and communities are important in the life of the Church because they allow for more intimate relationships, deeper study of faith, and mutual support.

Question: How can the Church support families in their spiritual development?

Answer: The Church can support families through family programs, workshops, counseling, support groups, and teaching directed at parents and children.

Question: What are the challenges for the Church in the context of modern technology and media?

Answer: Challenges for the Church include adapting to digital communication, safeguarding against misinformation, using media for evangelization, and maintaining authenticity in the virtual world.

Question: How can the Church contribute to dialogue and understanding between different cultures?

Answer: The Church can promote intercultural dialogue and understanding through education, cultural exchange, joint initiatives, and promoting respect for diversity.

Question: How does the Church deal with the challenges of religious pluralism?

Answer: The Church addresses religious pluralism through ecumenical and interfaith dialogue, respecting other beliefs while preserving its own identity and mission.

Question: What are the ways to engage youth in the life of the Church?

Answer: Ways to engage youth include youth groups, events, service programs, education tailored to their needs, and encouraging active participation.

Question: How can the Church support older and lonely individuals?

Answer: The Church can support older and lonely individuals through pastoral visits, support groups, charitable activities, and creating spaces for community and participation.

Question: How does the Church contribute to environmental protection and sustainable development?

Answer: The Church contributes to environmental protection through teaching about responsibility for creation, ecological initiatives, and promoting a sustainable lifestyle.

Question: What is the significance of volunteering and service in the Church?

Answer: Volunteering and service in the Church are significant because they allow for the practical expression of Christian love, community building, and serving those in need.

Question: How does the Church deal with the challenges of modernity, such as secularization?

Answer: The Church addresses the challenges of modernity through dialogue, adaptation, spiritual renewal, and active engagement with society.

Question: What are the methods of the Church in teaching and spiritual formation?

Answer: The methods of the Church in teaching and spiritual formation include sermons, Bible studies, retreats, workshops, courses, and various educational programs.

Question: What are the first steps to get involved in parish life?

Answer: The first steps include attending church services, getting familiar with parish activities, and talking to pastors or active members of the community about opportunities for involvement.

Question: Why is active participation in parish life important for a Christian?

Answer: Active participation in parish life strengthens faith, builds community, allows for service to others, and aids in personal spiritual development.

Question: What are the different forms of involvement in a parish?

Answer: Forms of involvement include liturgical service, charitable activities, participation in prayer groups, serving on parish councils, and organizing events.

Question: How can one find their place in the parish?

Answer: Finding one's place in the parish involves getting to know various groups and activities, recognizing one's talents and interests, and being open to suggestions and the needs of the community.

Question: Does involvement in the parish require special skills?

Answer: Not always; many forms of involvement only require a willingness to serve and a readiness to learn. Some roles may require special skills or experience.

Question: What are the benefits of participating in parish groups?

Answer: Participating in parish groups offers community, spiritual growth, opportunities for service, support, and friendships.

Question: How can families contribute to parish life?

Answer: Families can contribute by attending church services, engaging in family-oriented activities, participating in parish events, and serving as a family unit.

Question: What are the ways to encourage youth involvement in the parish?

Answer: Ways to encourage youth involvement include creating attractive youth programs, giving youth a role and a voice in the parish, organizing events aimed at youth, and providing mentorship.

Question: What is the significance of volunteering in the parish?

Answer: Volunteering in the parish is crucial because it allows for the practical expression of faith, supports parish activities, and builds a sense of community.

Question: How can one initiate a new activity or group in the parish?

Answer: Initiating a new activity requires discussions with pastors, assessing interest among parishioners, planning and organizing resources, and promoting the initiative.

Question: What are the challenges associated with involvement in parish life?

Answer: Challenges may include finding time, overcoming differences among parishioners, and adapting to changing parish needs.

Question: What is the importance of worship services and prayer meetings in parish life?

Answer: Worship services and prayer meetings are crucial

because they strengthen faith, build community, and provide a source of spiritual support.

Question: How can a parish support new members?

Answer: A parish can support new members through welcome programs, mentoring, sharing information about activities and groups, and creating a friendly atmosphere.

Question: What are the ways to promote unity and cooperation in a parish?

Answer: Ways to promote unity include organizing joint events, fostering dialogue and understanding, and actively involving various groups in parish life.

Question: What are the ways to develop leadership skills in the parish?

Answer: Developing leadership skills can be achieved through training, mentorship, active involvement in parish projects, and learning from experienced leaders.

Question: How can a parish engage seniors in its activities?

Answer: A parish can engage seniors by creating programs tailored to their needs, encouraging them to share their experience and wisdom, and offering roles that align with their abilities.

Question: What is the significance of music and singing in parish life?

Answer: Music and singing are of great significance in parish life because they enrich the liturgy, help express faith, and build community.

Question: How can technology be integrated into parish activities?

Answer: Technology can be integrated through online broadcasts, the use of social media for communication, organizing virtual meetings, and using apps for managing activities.

Question: What are the methods for effective communication in the parish?

Answer: Effective communication in the parish involves clear and open information sharing, using various communication channels, and encouraging feedback from parishioners.

Question: What are the ways to build a strong and healthy parish community?

Answer: Ways to build a community include organizing inclusive events, promoting openness and acceptance, and creating spaces for conversations and relationship-building.

Question: How can a parish support families in times of difficulty?

Answer: A parish can support families in difficulty through counseling, material assistance, prayer, and creating a support network.

Question: What are the challenges associated with maintaining a parish, and how can they be overcome?

Answer: Challenges related to maintaining a parish include finances, resource management, and adapting to changing needs. They can be overcome through effective management, parishioner engagement, and seeking new sources of support.

Question: How can a parish promote social responsibility and service to others?

Answer: A parish can promote social responsibility by organizing charitable actions, educating about social justice, and encouraging volunteering.

Question: What are the ways to involve parishioners in decisions related to the parish?

Answer: Ways to involve parishioners include creating parish councils, organizing consultation meetings, and encouraging participation in surveys and discussions.

Question: How can a parish care for the environment and promote sustainable development?

Answer: A parish can care for the environment by promoting eco-friendly practices, organizing educational events on environmental protection, and implementing sustainable solutions in its activities.

Question: What are the methods for attracting new members to the parish?

Answer: Methods for attracting new members include openness and hospitality, promoting parish activities in the local community, and creating attractive programs for various age groups.

Question: How can a parish support individuals in a crisis of faith?

Answer: A parish can support individuals in a crisis of faith through individual conversations, support groups, access to spiritual counseling, and offering educational materials.

Question: What is the significance of bearing witness to faith in parish life?

Answer: Bearing witness to faith is crucial because it inspires others, strengthens the community, and is an expression of personal experience with God.

Question: What are the ways to engage young adults in parish life?

Answer: Engaging young adults can be achieved through creating youth groups, organizing events tailored to their age group, and offering leadership roles in the parish.

Question: How can the parish support seniors and the elderly?

Answer: The parish can support seniors and the elderly by organizing social gatherings, providing transportation to religious services, and offering home visits.

Question: What is the significance of intergenerational cooperation in the parish?

Answer: Promoting intergenerational cooperation can be achieved through organizing joint projects, creating discussion groups, and encouraging the sharing of experiences between different age groups.

Question: How can the parish involve individuals with disabilities?

Answer: Involving individuals with disabilities requires adapting spaces and events to their needs, creating special programs, and promoting their active participation.

Question: What are the methods for encouraging regular giving and financial support to the parish?

Answer: Encouraging financial support can be achieved through transparently communicating the parish's needs, organizing fundraising efforts, and educating about the importance of giving.

Question: How can the parish respond to social and humanitarian crises?

Answer: The parish can respond to crises by organizing humanitarian aid, offering prayers for the affected, and collaborating with charitable organizations.

Question: What is the importance of interfaith and ecumenical dialogue in the parish?

Answer: Interfaith and ecumenical dialogue are important as they promote understanding and peace between different faith communities and enrich one's spiritual perspective.

Question: How can the parish promote mental health and emotional support?

Answer: Promoting mental health can be achieved through organizing workshops, providing counseling services, and creating safe spaces for sharing experiences.

Question: What are the methods for incorporating new technologies into parish activities?

Answer: Incorporating new technologies involves using social media, mobile apps, and online tools for communication, education, and event organization.

Question: How can the parish care for sustainable development and the environment?

Answer: Caring for the environment can be achieved by promoting sustainable practices, organizing educational events on environmental protection, and implementing eco-friendly solutions in parish activities.

Question: What are the ways to build relationships with the local community?

Answer: Building relationships with the local community can be achieved by organizing open events, collaborating with local organizations, and engaging in local initiatives.

Question: How can the parish support the religious education of children and youth?

Answer: Supporting religious education can be achieved through organizing catechesis, workshops, youth groups, and involving parents in the educational process.

Question: What is the significance of volunteering in parish life?

Answer: Volunteering is significant as it builds community, develops skills, and is an expression of Christian service.

Question: How can the parish promote a culture of gratitude and recognition?

Answer: Promoting a culture of gratitude can be achieved by regularly thanking and appreciating the involvement of parishioners, organizing ceremonies and events to acknowledge the contributions of volunteers, and cultivating an attitude of gratitude in communication and parish activities.

Question: What is ecumenism and why is it important in Christianity?

Answer: Ecumenism is the pursuit of unity among different Christian denominations, aiming to overcome divisions and provide a common witness of faith.

Question: What are the main goals of the ecumenical movement?

Answer: The main goals of the ecumenical movement are to promote dialogue between churches, mutual understanding and respect, and joint efforts for justice and peace.

Question: How can different Christian denominations work together despite doctrinal differences?

Answer: They can collaborate through dialogue, joint charitable and educational projects, and participation in ecumenical worship services and events.

Question: What are the challenges associated with ecumenism?

Answer: Challenges include doctrinal differences, historical divisions, and variations in the interpretation of Scripture and tradition.

Question: What is the significance of ecumenical dialogue for reconciliation between churches?

Answer: Ecumenical dialogue is crucial for understanding and overcoming divisions, leading to deeper reconciliation and cooperation.

Question: How can individual Christians contribute to ecumenism?

Answer: By participating in ecumenical events, praying for unity, and promoting openness and dialogue in their communities.

Question: What are examples of successful ecumenical initiatives?

Answer: Examples include joint worship services, charitable projects, and inter-church discussion groups.

Question: What is the significance of the Week of Prayer for Christian Unity?

Answer: It is an annual event that promotes prayer and actions for Christian unity worldwide.

Question: How does ecumenism affect the relationships between churches and society?

Answer: Through joint actions, churches can have a more effective and unified impact on society, promoting values such as peace, justice, and neighborly love.

Question: What are the differences between ecumenism and interreligious dialogue?

Answer: Ecumenism focuses on unity among Christians, while interreligious dialogue involves conversations and cooperation between different religions.

Question: How can ecumenism contribute to the development of theology?

Answer: By exchanging thoughts and experiences, ecumenism can enrich the understanding of theology and open up new perspectives.

Question: What are the benefits of ecumenical biblical studies?

Answer: These studies allow for a deeper understanding of Scripture through diverse perspectives and a shared exploration of its meaning.

Question: How does ecumenism impact Christian missions?

Answer: Joint missions can be more effective and unified, positively influencing the Christian witness in the world.

Question: What is the significance of ecumenism in the context of global challenges such as poverty and climate change?

Answer: Christian cooperation can more effectively address global issues by promoting solidarity and joint action for the common good.

Question: What are the main obstacles to achieving Christian unity?

Answer: The main obstacles are doctrinal differences, historical divisions, and different interpretations of liturgical practices and sacraments.

Question: How can ecumenism impact local Christian communities?

Answer: It can contribute to mutual understanding, cooperation in social and charitable activities, and the building of stronger communities.

Question: What methods can be used to overcome doctrinal barriers in ecumenism?

Answer: Methods include theological dialogue, mutual training and education, and joint study of Scripture.

Question: How can ecumenism contribute to peace and social justice?

Answer: Through joint actions and witness, Christians can more effectively promote values of peace and justice in society.

Question: What are examples of international ecumenical initiatives?

Answer: Examples include the World Council of Churches, the Week of Prayer for Christian Unity, and various international ecumenical conferences.

Question: What is the significance of ecumenism in the context of globalization?

Answer: In the context of globalization, ecumenism promotes global Christian solidarity and joint action in the face of global challenges.

Question: How does ecumenism affect the relationships between churches and governments?

Answer: It can lead to better cooperation and dialogue with authorities, as well as joint efforts in support of human rights and religious freedom.

Question: What are the challenges of ecumenism in the context of modern technology and social media?

Answer: Challenges include managing diversity of opinions and information, and using new media to promote dialogue and unity.

Question: How can ecumenism contribute to the development of religious education?

Answer: It can enrich educational programs with diverse Christian perspectives and promote mutual understanding among followers of different traditions.

Question: What methods can be used to promote ecumenism among youth?

Answer: Methods include ecumenical youth camps, workshops, and social projects that engage young people in dialogue and cooperation.

Question: How does ecumenism impact the development of moral theology?

Answer: Shared reflection on ethical challenges can lead to a deeper understanding of Christian morality and its application in daily life.

Question: What is the significance of ecumenism in

the context of ecological challenges?

Answer: Joint Christian actions can more effectively promote environmental care and responsibility for creation.

Question: How can ecumenism influence the spiritual development of individual Christians?

Answer: Through meetings and the exchange of experiences with followers of other traditions, Christians can enrich their spiritual lives and understanding of faith.

Question: What are the prospects for the future development of ecumenism?

Answer: Prospects include further dialogue development, greater involvement of young people, and joint actions addressing global challenges.

Question: What are the main ecumenical challenges in the 21st century?

Answer: These challenges include growing secularism, cultural and social differences, and the need to adapt to a changing world.

Question: How can ecumenism contribute to the resolution of religious conflicts?

Answer: Through promoting dialogue and understanding, ecumenism can help ease tensions and build bridges between divided communities.

Question: What are examples of successful ecumenical initiatives at the local level?

Answer: Examples include joint charitable projects, ecumenical prayer groups, and organizing shared cultural events.

Question: How does ecumenism impact the understanding of sacraments in different Christian traditions?

Answer: Ecumenical dialogue can lead to a deeper understanding of different interpretations of sacraments and their significance in the life of faith.

Question: What are the ecumenical challenges in the context of migration and global population movement?

Answer: These challenges include integrating believers from different traditions into local communities and promoting mutual understanding and respect.

Question: How can ecumenism contribute to the development of Christian missions?

Answer: Joint missions can be more effective in conveying the Christian message and serving those in need.

Question: What is the significance of ecumenism in the context of growing religious pluralism?

Answer: It promotes mutual understanding and respect between different Christian traditions, which is crucial in a pluralistic world.

Question: How does ecumenism impact the development of liturgical theology?

Answer: Shared reflection on liturgy can lead to a deeper understanding of the diversity of worship and its significance in the life of the Church.

Question: What methods can be used to promote Christian unity among children and youth?

Answer: Methods include ecumenical educational

programs, joint social projects, and youth initiatives that promote dialogue and understanding.

Question: How can ecumenism influence the development of pastoral theology?

Answer: Collaborative work on pastoral issues can lead to a better understanding of the needs and challenges of contemporary Christians.

Question: What is the significance of ecumenism in the context of challenges posed by new religious movements?

Answer: It can help understand and respond to the challenges posed by new movements while promoting solidarity and cooperation among traditional churches.

Question: How does ecumenism impact the development of social theology?

Answer: Joint reflection on the social aspects of faith can lead to a deeper understanding of the role of the Church in the world.

Question: What are the prospects for ecumenism in the context of growing individualization of faith?

Answer: The challenge is to find ways to promote community and unity among Christians who increasingly express their faith in individual ways.

Question: How can ecumenism contribute to the spiritual renewal of the Church?

Answer: Through shared search for truth and spiritual depth, ecumenism can inspire renewal and deepening of spiritual life in various Christian communities.

Section 7: Practical and Life Questions - Applying Christian Teachings in Professional and Public Life

Question: What are the Christian ethical principles in business?

Answer: These principles include honesty, justice, responsibility, respect for others, and working for the common good.

Question: How can Christians witness their faith in the workplace?

Answer: By practicing ethical behavior, honesty, compassion, and setting a good example in their daily interactions.

Question: What are Christian approaches to conflict management in the workplace?

Answer: These approaches include active listening, seeking just solutions, forgiveness, and avoiding gossip or judgment.

Question: How does Christianity influence leadership approaches?

Answer: The Christian approach to leadership is based on service, humility, responsibility, and caring for the well-being of employees.

Question: How can Christians deal with unethical practices in the workplace?

Answer: By speaking the truth, avoiding participation in unethical actions, and reporting wrongdoing to the appropriate authorities.

Question: What are Christian principles in making business decisions?

Answer: These principles include honesty, justice, considering the impact of decisions on others, and seeking ethical solutions.

Question: How can Christians promote social justice in their industry?

Answer: By advocating for equality, fair employment practices, and supporting sustainable development.

Question: What are Christian approaches to financial management in business?

Answer: These approaches include honest resource management, avoiding greed, and investing ethically and responsibly.

Question: How can Christians integrate faith with their professional careers?

Answer: By choosing ethical career paths, applying faith principles in daily decisions, and being vocal about their values.

Question: How does Christianity influence the approach to competition in business?

Answer: It promotes fair competition, respect for competitors, and avoiding unethical practices.

Question: How can Christians contribute to the ethical development of their industry?

Answer: By actively participating in industry organizations, promoting ethical standards, and sharing knowledge.

Question: What are Christian principles in dealing with clients and business partners?

Answer: These principles include honesty, transparency, respect, and building long-lasting, ethical relationships.

Question: How can Christians cope with market pressure and societal expectations?

Answer: By staying true to their values, avoiding ethical compromises, and seeking support within their faith community.

Question: What are Christian approaches to balancing professional and personal life?

Answer: These approaches include setting priorities aligned with faith values, taking care of one's health and family relationships, and making time for spiritual life.

Question: How does Christianity influence the approach to teamwork and collaboration?

Answer: It promotes values such as mutual respect, cooperation, empathy, and supporting each other in pursuit of common goals.

Question: How can Christians contribute to creating a positive organizational culture?

Answer: By promoting ethical behaviors, building trust, and creating an environment based on mutual respect and support.

Question: What are the Christian principles in approaching human resource management?

Answer: These principles include justice, equality, respect for the dignity of every person, and nurturing employee development.

Question: How can Christians promote ethics in marketing and advertising?

Answer: By avoiding deception, promoting truth and honesty in communication, and respecting the dignity of the audience.

Question: How does Christianity influence the approach to negotiation and business contracts?

Answer: It promotes honesty, transparency, seeking fair terms for all parties, and avoiding manipulation.

Question: How can Christians deal with ethical pressure in a corporate environment?

Answer: By sticking to their values, seeking support from fellow Christians, and being prepared to face the ethical consequences of their decisions.

Question: What are the Christian principles in crisis management?

Answer: These principles include honesty, transparency, accountability, and minimizing harm to all stakeholders.

Question: How can Christians contribute to sustainable development in their industry?

Answer: By promoting sustainable practices, caring for the environment, and pursuing the long-term common good.

Question: How does Christianity influence the approach to innovation and change in business?

Answer: It promotes an ethical approach to innovation, respecting the impact of changes on employees and the community, and pursuing progress in alignment with values.

Question: How can Christians promote equality and diversity in the workplace?

Answer: By taking active steps towards equality, combating discrimination, and creating a work environment that respects diversity.

Question: What are the Christian principles in risk management?

Answer: These principles include prudence, responsible risk management, and avoiding unnecessary risk at the expense of others.

Question: How can Christians deal with ethical challenges in the digital era?

Answer: By promoting digital ethics, protecting privacy, and using technology responsibly.

Question: How does Christianity influence the approach to corporate social responsibility?

Answer: It encourages active engagement in addressing social issues, investing in the community, and working for the common good.

Question: How can Christians integrate their faith with personal and professional development?

Answer: By continually striving for personal development in line with Christian values and finding ways to use their talents and skills in service to others.

Question: How does Christianity influence the approach to balancing professional success and moral values?

Answer: It promotes the pursuit of success without losing sight of values such as honesty, empathy, and social responsibility.

Question: How can Christians use their professional positions to promote social justice?

Answer: By actively working for equality, conducting business with integrity, and getting involved in social and charitable initiatives.

Question: What are the Christian principles in managing time and priorities at work?

Answer: These principles include effective time management, setting priorities in line with faith values, and maintaining a balance between work and personal life.

Question: How can Christians deal with ethical dilemmas at work?

Answer: By seeking guidance from spiritual mentors, praying for wisdom, and finding solutions that align with Christian values.

Question: How does Christianity influence the approach to managing stress and pressure in the workplace?

Answer: It promotes stress-coping techniques based on prayer, meditation, and trust in God, as well as encourages seeking support within the faith community.

Question: How can Christians contribute to promoting ethics in remote work environments?

Answer: By maintaining high standards of integrity, transparent communication, and taking responsibility for their tasks.

Question: What are the Christian principles in

approaching professional development and advancement?

Answer: These principles include pursuing development in alignment with ethical values, avoiding unfair competition, and promoting collaboration.

Question: How can Christians integrate faith with corporate ethics?

Answer: By actively participating in creating ethical standards within the organization and promoting values such as honesty and responsibility.

Question: How does Christianity influence the approach to diversity and inclusion in the workplace?

Answer: It promotes respect for diversity, equal opportunities, and creating a workplace that is open and welcoming to all.

Question: How can Christians promote sustainable development in their organizations?

Answer: By initiating and supporting sustainable development projects, caring for the environment, and promoting responsible resource management.

Question: What are the Christian principles in managing change within an organization?

Answer: These principles include honesty, transparency, concern for employees' well-being, and seeking changes aligned with Christian values.

Question: How can Christians handle ethical conflicts in the workplace?

Answer: By seeking peaceful solutions, engaging in respectful dialogue, and striving for solutions that align with Christian values.

Question: How does Christianity influence the approach to talent management and employee development?

Answer: It promotes talent development with a spirit of service, investing in employee growth, and creating a work environment conducive to development.

Question: How can Christians use their skills and knowledge to serve others in the workplace?

Answer: By sharing knowledge and experience, mentoring, and engaging in activities that support the development of others.

Question: What are the basic principles of Christian child-rearing?

Answer: The basic principles include teaching love, respect, honesty, responsibility, and faith in God.

Question: How can parents introduce their children to prayer and spirituality?

Answer: Through shared prayers, reading biblical stories, and participating in church life.

Question: What are the methods for teaching children Christian values in everyday life?

Answer: These methods include setting a good example, having discussions about values, and involving children in charitable activities.

Question: How to address children's questions about God and faith?

Answer: By patiently and understandably explaining,

encouraging them to ask questions, and seeking answers together.

Question: How to raise children with tolerance and respect for other religions?

Answer: By teaching about religious diversity, demonstrating respect for other beliefs, and promoting interfaith dialogue.

Question: What are Christian approaches to disciplining and shaping a child's character?

Answer: These approaches are based on love, consistency, and teaching by example rather than punishment.

Question: How to incorporate biblical teachings into the family's daily life?

Answer: Through daily Bible reading, discussions about its content, and applying its teachings in family life.

Question: How to encourage youth to actively participate in church life?

Answer: By involving them in youth groups, church volunteering, and organizing engaging religious events.

Question: How to address the doubts and questions of youth about faith?

Answer: Through open discussions, support in seeking answers, and encouraging independent thinking.

Question: How to teach youth social and charitable responsibility?

Answer: By organizing joint charity actions, teaching the importance of helping others, and setting an example through one's own actions.

Question: What are the methods for teaching youth about sexual morality in line with Christian values?

Answer: These methods include open and respectful discussions, education about the body and sexuality, and teaching the importance of love and commitment.

Question: How to raise children and youth with ecumenism and openness to other faiths?

Answer: By educating them about different Christian traditions, organizing interfaith meetings, and promoting dialogue and understanding.

Question: How to encourage youth's personal spiritual development?

Answer: By supporting them in finding their own spiritual path, encouraging participation in retreats and workshops, and discussing the importance of spirituality.

Question: How can Christian values help youth cope with the challenges of the modern world?

Answer: By teaching the power of faith, hope, and love in the face of difficulties, and promoting attitudes based on compassion and responsibility.

Question: What are Christian approaches to educating youth about sexuality?

Answer: These approaches are based on teaching respect for one's own body, the importance of love and commitment, and sexual responsibility.

Question: How can parents teach children about the importance of mercy and forgiveness?

Answer: By setting an example of forgiveness, discussing the importance of mercy in Christian life, and encouraging the practice of these values.

Question: How to raise children with a spirit of serving others and volunteering?

Answer: By involving them in charitable activities, teaching the importance of helping those in need, and setting an example through one's own actions.

Question: How to teach youth about the importance of honesty and integrity?

Answer: Through discussions about the significance of these values, setting an example of honest behavior, and encouraging them to act in accordance with moral principles.

Question: What methods are there for teaching children about the importance of prayer and its role in life?

Answer: These methods include shared prayers, teaching about various forms of prayer, and encouraging personal prayer.

Question: How to raise children with respect for the world and the environment?

Answer: By teaching responsibility for creation, promoting ecological attitudes, and engaging in actions to protect the environment.

Question: How to address children's questions about death and the afterlife?

Answer: By patiently explaining Christian views on these topics, providing emotional support, and discussing hope and eternity.

Question: How to teach youth about the importance of

financial responsibility?

Answer: By educating them about money management, teaching the importance of giving and sharing with others, and promoting savings and wise financial practices.

Question: What are Christian approaches to teaching about diversity and acceptance?

Answer: These approaches include teaching about the equality of all people before God, promoting tolerance and understanding, and combating discrimination.

Question: How to raise children with respect for Christian traditions and history?

Answer: By teaching about the history of the Church, saints, and religious traditions, and participating in church ceremonies.

Question: How to encourage youth to actively seek their own spiritual path?

Answer: By supporting their search, encouraging participation in various forms of spirituality, and discussing the importance of a personal relationship with God.

Question: How to teach children about the importance of teamwork and cooperation?

Answer: By organizing group activities, teaching the importance of cooperation and mutual support, and setting an example through joint actions.

Question: How to address youth's questions about doubts and crises of faith?

Answer: Through open conversations, support in seeking answers, and ensuring that doubts are a natural part of spiritual growth.

Question: How to raise children with a spirit of love and empathy towards others?

Answer: By teaching the importance of loving one's neighbor, setting an example of empathetic behavior, and encouraging help and understanding for others.

Question: What are Christian approaches to discipline and setting boundaries for children?

Answer: These approaches are based on love and respect, establishing clear and consistent boundaries, and teaching about consequences and responsibility.

Question: How to teach youth about the importance of honesty and truthfulness?

Answer: Through discussions about the value of truth, setting an example of honest behavior, and encouraging them to be truthful even in difficult situations.

Question: How to raise children with respect for cultural and religious differences?

Answer: By educating them about the diversity of the world, promoting openness and understanding, and teaching the value of loving one's neighbor regardless of differences.

Question: How to teach children about the importance of compassion and helping others?

Answer: By involving them in charitable activities, discussing the importance of empathy, and setting an example of helping those in need.

Question: What methods are there for teaching youth about the importance of patience and perseverance?

Answer: Methods include discussions about the value of patience, encouraging them to overcome challenges, and setting an example of perseverance in the face of adversity.

Question: How to teach children about the importance of humility and avoiding pride?

Answer: Through discussions about the value of humility, teaching about the pitfalls of pride, and setting an example of humble behavior.

Question: How to address children's questions about evil and suffering in the world?

Answer: By discussing the Christian understanding of evil and suffering, teaching about the importance of love and hope, and providing support during difficult times.

Question: How to teach youth about the importance of social responsibility?

Answer: By educating them about social issues, encouraging them to get involved in activities for others, and teaching Christian social ethics.

Question: What are Christian approaches to teaching about the importance of tolerance and acceptance?

Answer: These approaches include teaching about the equality of all people, promoting understanding and acceptance of differences, and combating prejudice.

Question: How to raise children with respect for life and its sanctity?

Answer: By teaching about the value of life from conception to natural death, promoting respect for all beings, and discussing the importance of protecting life.

Question: How to encourage youth to actively participate in church life?

Answer: By involving them in parish activities, discussing the importance of the faith community, and setting an example of active religious life.

Question: How to teach children about the importance of love and respect within the family?

Answer: Through discussions about family values, setting an example of love and respect in family relationships, and encouraging the expression of feelings and support within the family.

Question: How to address youth's questions about interpersonal relationships and friendships?

Answer: By discussing the importance of healthy relationships, teaching values such as loyalty and trust, and providing support in building positive relationships.

Question: How to raise children with a sense of responsibility for their decisions and actions?

Answer: By teaching about the consequences of choices, encouraging independence and responsibility, and providing support in learning from experiences.

Question: What are the Christian principles of managing personal finances?

Answer: These principles are based on honesty, prudence, avoiding excessive debt, and sharing with those in need.

Question: How does Christianity approach saving and investing?

Answer: It emphasizes the importance of wise and ethical investing, taking into account future needs but without greed or excessive attachment to material possessions.

Question: What are the Christian guidelines for giving alms and helping the needy?

Answer: These guidelines encourage generosity, supporting the poor and needy, and giving from the heart, not for show.

Question: How should Christians approach the issue of debts and loans?

Answer: One should avoid excessive debt, be honest in repaying debts, and be prudent in lending money.

Question: What are the Christian principles for managing family wealth?

Answer: These principles are based on fair distribution, responsible management, and passing on spiritual values along with material wealth.

Question: How does Christianity approach the issue of wealth and its use?

Answer: It emphasizes that wealth should be used for the common good, avoiding excessive attachment to material possessions.

Question: What are the Christian guidelines for financial planning for the future?

Answer: These guidelines encourage prudent planning, securing the future of the family, but without excessive worry or anxiety about the future.

Question: How should Christians approach the issue of ethical investments?

Answer: They should avoid investments in industries that

conflict with Christian values and seek opportunities for investments that promote the common good.

Question: What are the Christian principles for managing resources in business?

Answer: These principles are based on honesty, justice, caring for the well-being of employees and customers, and social responsibility.

Question: How does Christianity approach the issue of consumerism?

Answer: It emphasizes the need for moderation, avoiding excessive consumerism, and appreciating non-material values.

Question: What are the Christian guidelines for sharing resources with the church and charitable organizations?

Answer: These guidelines encourage regular and generous support for the work of the church and charitable organizations as an expression of gratitude to God and care for others.

Question: How should Christians approach the issue of wills and inheritance?

Answer: They should plan inheritance wisely, ensuring the needs of the family while also considering the possibility of supporting charitable causes.

Question: What are the Christian principles for managing financial crises?

Answer: These principles are based on maintaining faith and hope, seeking wise solutions, and being open to community support.

Question: How does Christianity approach the issue of poverty and social inequality?

Answer: It emphasizes the need for active advocacy for social justice, support for the poor, and efforts to reduce inequality.

Question: How does Christianity deal with the issue of greed and the desire for possession?

Answer: Christianity teaches to avoid greed, promoting contentment with what one has and focusing on spiritual values over material ones.

Question: How should Christians approach the issue of donations and offerings?

Answer: Donations and offerings should be given from the heart, as an expression of gratitude to God and concern for the needs of others, without expecting rewards.

Question: What are the Christian principles for managing finances in marriage?

Answer: These principles are based on mutual respect, transparency, making financial decisions together, and avoiding conflicts related to money.

Question: How does Christianity approach the issue of poverty and helping the poor?

Answer: Christianity teaches that helping the poor is a fundamental duty, emphasizing mercy and solidarity with those in need.

Question: What are the Christian guidelines for ethical business management?

Answer: These guidelines emphasize honesty, social responsibility, fair treatment of employees and customers, and avoiding unethical practices.

Question: How should Christians approach the issue of earning and spending money?

Answer: They should earn money honestly, spend it prudently, avoid excessive materialism, and promote a balance between personal needs and supporting others.

Question: What are the Christian principles for investing in education and personal development?

Answer: These principles encourage investing in education as a means of personal growth and better serving the community, while also considering spiritual values.

Question: How does Christianity approach the issue of luxury and comfort?

Answer: It emphasizes moderation and avoiding excessive luxury, encouraging sharing excess with those in need.

Question: What are the Christian guidelines for managing time and resources?

Answer: These guidelines emphasize the importance of wise time management, balancing work with spiritual life, and using resources responsibly.

Question: How should Christians approach the issue of philanthropy and patronage?

Answer: They should engage in philanthropy and patronage out of a sense of mercy and a desire to support the common good, not for personal glory.

Question: What are the Christian principles for managing natural resources?

Answer: These principles are based on respect for

creation, responsible management of natural resources, and efforts to protect the environment.

Question: How does Christianity approach the issue of ethics in advertising and marketing?

Answer: It emphasizes the need for honesty, transparency, and avoiding manipulation in advertising and marketing.

Question: What are the Christian guidelines for managing financial risk?

Answer: These guidelines encourage prudent risk management, avoiding unnecessary risks, and trusting in God's providence in uncertain situations.

Question: How should Christians approach the issue of social responsibility in business?

Answer: They should strive to conduct business ethically, promote the common good, justice, and environmental stewardship.

Question: How does Christianity approach the issue of saving and investing money?

Answer: Christianity encourages prudent saving and ethical investing, considering responsibility for future generations and aiding those in need.

Question: How should Christians approach the issue of debts and loans?

Answer: They should avoid excessive debt, be honest in repaying debts, and be cautious in lending, always respecting the dignity of the other person.

Question: What are the Christian principles for managing family wealth?

Answer: These principles emphasize fair and responsible management of family wealth, with the well-being of all family members and future generations in mind.

Question: How does Christianity approach the issue of estate planning and inheritances?

Answer: It stresses the importance of fair and honest distribution of wealth, respecting the wishes of the deceased and the needs of all heirs.

Question: What are the Christian guidelines for ethical business management?

Answer: These guidelines include honesty, social responsibility, ethical treatment of employees and customers, and a commitment to sustainable development.

Question: How should Christians approach the issue of consumerism?

Answer: They should avoid excessive consumerism, promote moderation, be grateful for what they have, and share with those in need.

Question: What are the Christian principles for investing in health and well-being?

Answer: These principles encourage caring for physical, mental, and spiritual health as a gift from God, with responsibility for one's well-being and helping others.

Question: How does Christianity approach the issue of luxury and the consumption of luxury goods?

Answer: It emphasizes moderation, avoiding excessive luxury, encouraging the sharing of resources, and focusing on spiritual values.

Question: What are the Christian guidelines for managing leisure time and recreation?

Answer: These guidelines stress the importance of balancing work and rest, spending time with family and friends, and engaging in church and community activities.

Question: How should Christians approach the issue of investing in art and culture?

Answer: They should invest in art and culture that promotes Christian values, enriches spirituality, and serves the common good.

Question: What are the Christian principles for managing resources in crisis situations?

Answer: These principles emphasize solidarity, sharing with those in need, and responsible resource management in difficult circumstances.

Question: How does Christianity approach the issue of ethics in international trade?

Answer: It emphasizes fair trade, social justice, and promoting economic development in a sustainable and ethical manner.

Question: What are the Christian guidelines for managing personal and professional risk?

Answer: These guidelines encourage prudent decision-making, avoiding unnecessary risks, and trusting in God's providence in uncertain situations.

Question: How should Christians approach the issue of social and ethical responsibility in their professional lives?

Answer: They should strive for ethical conduct at work,

promoting honesty, justice, and social responsibility, always respecting human dignity.

Section 8: Questions about Contemporary Challenges - The Role of Christianity in the World of Modern Technology and Social Media

Question: How should Christianity relate to the growing role of social media in everyday life?

Answer: Christianity encourages conscious and responsible use of social media, promoting values such as truth, respect, and the building of positive relationships.

Question: How can Christians use technology to spread faith and Christian values?

Answer: By creating and sharing inspirational content, organizing virtual meetings and discussions, and using digital platforms for religious and spiritual education.

Question: What are the ethical challenges related to modern technologies for Christians?

Answer: These challenges include privacy protection, avoiding misinformation, ethical use of data, and maintaining a balance between digital and real life.

Question: How can Christianity contribute to the healthy development of technology?

Answer: By promoting ethical standards in the design and use of technology, and encouraging the creation of technologies that support the common good and human dignity.

Question: How should Christians deal with the negative aspects of social media, such as cyberbullying and hate?

Answer: By promoting a culture of respect and empathy online, actively combating hate speech, and educating about safe internet use.

Question: How can Christianity influence the development of artificial intelligence and robotics?

Answer: By promoting ethical principles in the design and use of AI, with an emphasis on respecting human dignity and preventing abuses.

Question: What are Christian perspectives on privacy and data security in the digital age?

Answer: Christianity emphasizes the importance of privacy protection as a part of personal dignity, encouraging responsible management of personal and digital data.

Question: How can Christians use technology to promote interreligious and intercultural dialogue?

Answer: By creating platforms for the exchange of thoughts and experiences, organizing virtual meetings and conferences, and promoting mutual understanding and respect.

Question: What are the challenges related to the digital spread of false information, and how can Christians combat them?

Answer: By educating about critical thinking and source verification, actively countering misinformation, and promoting truth and transparency.

Question: How can Christianity contribute to the development of ethical standards in video games and digital entertainment?

Answer: By promoting content that aligns with Christian values, encouraging the creation of positive and educational games, and critically evaluating entertainment content.

Question: How can Christians use technology to support the needs of the needy and marginalized groups?

Answer: By creating applications and platforms that support charitable activities, organizing online social campaigns, and using technology for education and integration.

Question: How can Christianity influence the development of technology for environmental protection?

Answer: By promoting sustainable development technologies, supporting environmental initiatives, and educating about responsibility for creation.

Question: What are the Christian principles regarding the use of technology in education and learning?

Answer: These principles emphasize the ethical use of technology in education, promoting the integral development of the individual, and maintaining a balance between knowledge and moral values.

Question: How can Christianity contribute to the healthy development of digital media and

communication?

Answer: By promoting ethical standards in media, encouraging the creation of constructive and educational content, and actively participating in digital public discourse.

Question: How can Christianity help in dealing with addiction to social media and technology?

Answer: By promoting a healthy balance between digital and real-life, encouraging mindful use of technology, and offering spiritual support for individuals struggling with addiction.

Question: How can Christians use technology to promote peace and conflict resolution?

Answer: By creating platforms for dialogue and mediation, promoting content that advocates peace and understanding, and using media for education on conflict resolution.

Question: What are Christian perspectives on anonymity and identity on the internet?

Answer: Christianity emphasizes the importance of authenticity and truthfulness, encouraging responsible self-presentation online and avoiding false identities.

Question: How can Christians use technology to support mission and evangelization?

Answer: By creating evangelistic content tailored to digital media, organizing virtual religious events, and using online platforms to reach a broader audience.

Question: How can Christianity influence the development of medical and biotechnological technologies?

Answer: By promoting ethical standards in research and development, with a focus on respecting the sanctity of life and human dignity.

Question: How can Christians use technology to promote social justice?

Answer: By using media to raise awareness about injustice, supporting social campaigns and initiatives, and using technology for mobilizing and organizing charitable actions.

Question: What are the Christian principles regarding the use of technology in religious education?

Answer: These principles include promoting the integral spiritual and intellectual development, using technology to facilitate access to religious education, and ensuring content aligns with Christian doctrine.

Question: How can Christianity contribute to the development of technologies for social integration?

Answer: By promoting technologies that support the integration of individuals from different backgrounds and cultures, and using media to bridge gaps between diverse social groups.

Question: How can Christians use technology to promote mental health and emotional support?

Answer: By creating platforms and applications offering spiritual and emotional support, organizing virtual support groups, and promoting a healthy lifestyle.

Question: How can Christianity influence the development of communication technologies?

Answer: By promoting technologies that facilitate communication and understanding among people, encouraging the creation of community-building content, and using media to spread Christian values.

Question: What are the Christian perspectives on using technology in charitable activities?

Answer: Christianity encourages the use of technology for effective organization of aid and support for the needy, promoting transparency in charitable work, and building a global network of solidarity.

Question: How can Christians use technology to promote a culture of life and environmental protection?

Answer: By using media for education on life and environmental protection, supporting ecological initiatives, and promoting sustainable resource use.

Question: What are the challenges related to the digital dissemination of religious content, and how can Christians address them?

Answer: These challenges include maintaining authenticity and accuracy of religious content, avoiding manipulation and misinformation, and promoting healthy digital religious discourse.

Question: How can Christianity contribute to the development of technologies supporting education and personal development?

Answer: By promoting technologies that facilitate access to education, support personal and spiritual development, and encourage lifelong learning and growth.

Question: How can Christianity influence the ethical use of artificial intelligence and robotics?

Answer: By promoting ethical standards in the design and

utilization of AI, with an emphasis on respecting human dignity and avoiding technological abuses.

Question: How can Christians use social media for community-building and support?

Answer: By creating online groups and forums that offer spiritual support, provide a space for sharing experiences, and foster relationships among believers.

Question: What are Christian perspectives on privacy and data security in the digital world?

Answer: Christianity emphasizes the importance of protecting privacy as a component of personal dignity, encouraging responsible data management and conscious use of technology.

Question: How can Christianity contribute to the development of technologies supporting health and well-being?

Answer: By promoting technologies that enhance the quality of life, support physical and mental health, and are accessible to all social strata.

Question: How can Christians use technology to promote education and social awareness?

Answer: By creating educational and informative content that promotes Christian values and raises awareness about important social issues.

Question: What are the Christian principles regarding the use of technology in missionary work?

Answer: These principles include respecting the cultures and traditions one interacts with and using technology in a way that supports rather than imposes the evangelical message.

Question: How can Christians use technology to promote international solidarity and humanitarian aid?

Answer: By using media to mobilize support for international aid initiatives and promoting technologies that facilitate the delivery of aid and assistance to those in need.

Question: How can Christianity influence the development of educational technologies, especially in developing countries?

Answer: By promoting technologies that are accessible and affordable for communities in developing countries, supporting education and development through technology.

Question: How can Christians use technology to promote global ecological awareness?

Answer: By using media to educate about climate change and environmental protection and promoting environmentally friendly technologies.

Question: What are Christian perspectives on using technology to promote a healthy lifestyle?

Answer: Christianity encourages the use of technology in a way that supports physical and spiritual health, promoting physical activity, healthy eating, and life balance.

Question: How can Christianity contribute to the development of technologies that support the integration of people with disabilities?

Answer: By promoting technologies tailored to the needs of people with disabilities, supporting their social and professional integration.

Question: How can Christians use technology to promote Christian culture and art?

Answer: By creating and promoting artistic and cultural content that reflects Christian values and using media to disseminate them.

Question: How can Christianity influence the development of technologies that support the development of local communities?

Answer: By promoting technologies that support local initiatives, strengthen social bonds, and promote community development at various levels.

Question: What is the Christian approach to climate change?

Answer: Christianity emphasizes the responsibility for caring for creation and encourages actions to protect the environment and promote sustainable development.

Question: How can Christians contribute to the fight against global warming?

Answer: By promoting and participating in environmental initiatives, educating about sustainable living, and supporting pro-environment policies.

Question: How does Christianity interpret pandemics, such as COVID-19, in the context of faith?

Answer: Pandemics can be seen as a call for reflection on human vulnerability, solidarity, and the need for spiritual and physical healing.

Question: What actions can Christians take to help during a pandemic?

Answer: Through volunteering, supporting those in need,

prayer, promoting a healthy lifestyle, and adhering to health guidelines.

Question: How can Christianity contribute to resolving international conflicts?

Answer: By promoting peace, reconciliation, intercultural and interreligious dialogue, and active engagement in diplomacy and humanitarian aid.

Question: How should Christians respond to humanitarian crises resulting from armed conflicts?

Answer: By supporting the victims of conflicts, praying for peace, supporting humanitarian organizations, and advocating for diplomatic solutions.

Question: What is the Christian stance on refugees and migrants?

Answer: Christianity teaches mercy and hospitality toward refugees and migrants, emphasizing the need for assistance and integration.

Question: How can Christians contribute to global food security?

Answer: By supporting sustainable food production, participating in food aid programs, and advocating for equitable access to resources.

Question: How can Christianity influence global efforts to reduce poverty?

Answer: Through charitable actions, education, support for sustainable development, and promotion of economic justice.

Question: How can Christians engage in biodiversity conservation?

Answer: By taking actions to protect the environment, supporting sustainable agriculture, and conserving endangered species.

Question: What is the Christian approach to natural resource management?

Answer: Christianity teaches responsible and sustainable resource management, with an emphasis on environmental protection for future generations.

Question: How can Christians contribute to the fight against global health issues?

Answer: By supporting global health initiatives, educating about public health, and participating in disease prevention programs.

Question: How can Christianity influence global education efforts?

Answer: By promoting access to education, supporting educational initiatives in developing countries, and emphasizing the role of education in social development.

Question: How can Christians engage in global gender equality efforts?

Answer: By promoting gender equality in local and global communities, supporting women's and girls' rights initiatives, and educating about gender equality.

Question: How does Christianity relate to the issue of social inequality in the world?

Answer: Christianity teaches the equality of all people before God and encourages actions for social justice and the reduction of inequality.

Question: How can Christians contribute to solving

the problem of world hunger?

Answer: By supporting food programs, promoting sustainable agriculture, and educating about food security.

Question: What is the Christian approach to the issue of access to clean water?

Answer: Christianity emphasizes the importance of access to clean water as a basic human right and encourages actions to ensure it.

Question: How can Christians engage in the protection of human rights?

Answer: By actively supporting human rights organizations, educating about human rights, and promoting their enforcement.

Question: How can Christianity contribute to global peace efforts?

Answer: By promoting dialogue, reconciliation, praying for peace, and supporting peace initiatives on the international stage.

Question: How can Christians respond to global ecological crises?

Answer: By actively participating in environmental protection efforts, promoting sustainable lifestyles, and supporting pro-environmental policies.

Question: What is the Christian stance on global trade and economics?

Answer: Christianity emphasizes the need for economic justice, fair trade, and corporate responsibility.

Question: How can Christians contribute to sustainable development?

Answer: By supporting sustainable development projects, promoting responsible consumerism, and educating about sustainable development.

Question: How does Christianity address the issue of overpopulation?

Answer: Christianity emphasizes responsible parenthood and encourages actions for sustainable demographic development.

Question: How can Christians engage in the protection of animals and the natural environment?

Answer: By taking actions to protect nature, supporting environmental organizations, and promoting humane treatment of animals.

Question: What is the Christian approach to sustainable energy issues?

Answer: Christianity encourages the search for and support of renewable energy sources and the promotion of energy efficiency.

Question: How can Christians contribute to global health education efforts?

Answer: By supporting educational programs, promoting a healthy lifestyle, and participating in health campaigns.

Question: How can Christianity influence global efforts for equality and social justice?

Answer: By actively engaging in actions for equality, supporting marginalized groups, and promoting social justice.

Question: How can Christians engage in actions to protect children's rights?

Answer: By supporting organizations working for children's rights, educating about child protection, and advocating for their rights at the local and global levels.

Question: How can Christianity contribute to combating global health issues such as pandemics?

Answer: By supporting global medical efforts, promoting health awareness, and participating in humanitarian actions.

Question: How can Christians respond to global migration crises?

Answer: By offering humanitarian aid, supporting migrant integration, and advocating for compassionate and just policies.

Question: What is the Christian stance on global warming and climate change?

Answer: Christianity encourages actions for environmental protection, promoting sustainable development, and responsible management of natural resources.

Question: How can Christians contribute to the global fight against poverty?

Answer: By supporting development programs, advocating for economic justice, and participating in social assistance initiatives.

Question: How does Christianity address the issue of illiteracy worldwide?

Answer: By promoting education, supporting teaching programs, and working to increase access to education.

Question: How can Christians engage in the protection of cultural diversity?

Answer: By promoting intercultural dialogue, respecting diversity, and supporting cultural heritage.

Question: What is the Christian approach to global food issues?

Answer: Christianity encourages actions for food security, support for sustainable agriculture, and combating food waste.

Question: How can Christians contribute to the protection of biodiversity?

Answer: By supporting environmental conservation, promoting sustainable use of natural resources, and educating about ecology.

Question: How does Christianity relate to the issue of natural resource depletion?

Answer: Christianity promotes responsible resource management, support for sustainable technologies, and environmental education.

Question: How can Christians respond to global challenges related to access to education?

Answer: By supporting educational initiatives, promoting equal access to education, and participating in educational projects.

Question: What is the Christian stance on global arms trade?

Answer: Christianity promotes peace and opposes the arms trade, which contributes to conflict and violence.

Question: How can Christians contribute to global efforts for gender equality?

Answer: By promoting gender equality, supporting women's rights, and participating in initiatives for gender equality.

Question: How can Christianity influence global environmental protection efforts?

Answer: By actively participating in environmental conservation, promoting sustainable lifestyles, and supporting pro-environmental policies.

Question: How can Christians engage in actions to protect animal rights?

Answer: By supporting organizations working for animal rights, promoting humane treatment of animals, and educating about animal protection.

Question: What are the main challenges for Christianity in the 21st century?

Answer: These challenges include secularization of society, interreligious dialogue, adaptation to modern technologies, and response to global crises.

Question: How can Christianity remain relevant in an increasingly globalized world?

Answer: By promoting universal values, adapting to cultural diversity, and actively participating in global dialogue.

Question: What are the prospects for the growth of Christianity in developing countries?

Answer: Growth can be driven by missionary work, local social initiatives, and responses to local needs.

Question: How can Christianity contribute to global peace and justice?

Answer: By promoting dialogue, supporting peace initiatives, and actively working for social justice.

Question: What is the place of Christianity in interreligious dialogue?

Answer: Christianity can play a bridging role, promoting mutual understanding and cooperation among different religions.

Question: How can Christianity respond to the growing individualism in society?

Answer: By emphasizing the value of community, service to others, and shared responsibility.

Question: How can Christianity adapt to changes in family structure?

Answer: By redefining its approach to marriage, parenthood, and family relationships in the context of contemporary social changes.

Question: What are the new forms of evangelization and mission in the digital age?

Answer: Utilizing social media, digital platforms, and modern technologies to spread the Christian message.

Question: How can Christianity address the ecological crisis?

Answer: By promoting ecological awareness, engaging in environmental protection efforts, and advocating for sustainable lifestyles.

Question: How can Christianity respond to challenges

related to modern technologies, such as artificial intelligence?

Answer: By adopting an ethical approach to technology, promoting humanistic values in technological development, and engaging in dialogue about the impact of technology on society.

Question: How can Christianity contribute to the development of education and science?

Answer: By supporting educational initiatives, promoting scientific and ethical values, and actively participating in scientific debates.

Question: What is the place of Christianity in popular culture?

Answer: Christianity can find its place in popular culture by creating content that reflects Christian values and engages a wide audience.

Question: How can Christianity counteract growing social and economic inequality?

Answer: By taking actions for social justice, supporting the poor and marginalized, and promoting equality.

Question: How can Christianity influence politics and public governance?

Answer: By actively participating in public life, promoting ethical standards in politics, and influencing decisions for the common good.

Question: How can Christianity contribute to solving the problem of poverty in the world?

Answer: Through charitable actions, support for sustainable development, and promotion of economic justice.

Question: How can Christianity respond to challenges related to migration and refugees?

Answer: By working towards integration, providing humanitarian support, and promoting a culture of hospitality.

Question: What is the place of Christianity in the human rights debate?

Answer: Christianity can be a strong advocate for human rights based on its ethical and moral principles.

Question: How can Christianity counteract extremism and intolerance?

Answer: By promoting dialogue, mutual understanding, and respect for diversity.

Question: How can Christianity influence education and the development of young people?

Answer: By offering educational programs based on Christian values and providing support to youth.

Question: How can Christianity contribute to combating discrimination and social inequalities?

Answer: Through active efforts for equality, support for marginalized groups, and promotion of inclusivity.

Question: What are Christian approaches to mental health and well-being?

Answer: By promoting a holistic approach to health, supporting individuals with mental health issues, and promoting well-being.

Question: How can Christianity respond to the growing challenges related to an aging society?

Answer: By taking actions for the elderly, supporting long-term care, and promoting dignity in old age.

Question: How can Christianity contribute to sustainable and just trade?

Answer: By promoting ethical business, fair trade, and responsible consumption.

Question: How can Christianity influence climate policy and environmental protection?

Answer: Through active efforts for environmental protection, promotion of sustainable development, and influencing climate policy.

Question: What is the place of Christianity in promoting peace and conflict resolution?

Answer: Christianity can act as a mediator, promoting dialogue and peaceful solutions in conflict situations.

Question: How can Christianity counteract issues related to addiction and abuse?

Answer: Through preventive actions, support for individuals with addiction issues, and promotion of a healthy lifestyle.

Question: How can Christianity influence technology and innovation?

Answer: By adopting an ethical approach to innovation, promoting technologies that serve the common good, and engaging in a dialogue about the impact of technology on society.

Question: How can Christianity contribute to global social justice?

Answer: Through actions to reduce inequalities, promotion of economic justice, and active participation in global social dialogue.

Question: How can Christianity contribute to the development of education and science in a global context?

Answer: By supporting educational initiatives that promote ethical and moral values and encouraging scientific research in a spirit of respect for life and the environment.

Question: How can Christianity respond to challenges related to global security and terrorism?

Answer: By promoting peace, interreligious dialogue, and international cooperation to combat extremism.

Question: What is the place of Christianity in the gender equality and women's rights debate?

Answer: Christianity can actively work for gender equality, promoting respect and dignity for every individual, regardless of gender.

Question: How can Christianity contribute to the development of a sustainable economy?

Answer: By promoting ethical business practices, economic justice, and responsible resource management.

Question: How can Christianity influence healthcare policy and healthcare provision?

Answer: By advocating for access to healthcare for all, promoting a healthy lifestyle, and upholding ethical standards in medicine.

Question: How can Christianity respond to challenges related to urbanization and urban life?

Answer: By working for urban communities, supporting those in difficult life situations, and promoting sustainable urban development.

Question: What are Christian approaches to global health issues, such as pandemics?

Answer: Through humanitarian actions, support for scientific research, and promoting solidarity in the face of global health challenges.

Question: How can Christianity contribute to the fight against global food problems?

Answer: By promoting sustainable food production and distribution, supporting local agriculture, and working to combat hunger.

Question: How can Christianity influence policies regarding refugees and migrants?

Answer: By advocating for the protection of refugee rights, promoting hospitality and integration, and actively participating in international dialogue.

Question: How can Christianity respond to challenges related to cultural diversity and social integration?

Answer: By promoting mutual respect, intercultural dialogue, and the acceptance of diversity.

Question: What is the place of Christianity in promoting sustainable development and environmental protection?

Answer: Christianity can actively participate in the global dialogue on sustainable development, promoting responsibility for the natural environment.

Question: How can Christianity contribute to the global debate on ethics in science and technology?

Answer: By engaging in discussions about the ethical aspects of science and technology, promoting responsible use of innovations.

Question: How can Christianity influence global discussions on education and the role of youth?

Answer: By engaging in shaping educational policy, supporting young people, and promoting Christian values in education.

Question: How can Christianity contribute to building global peace and justice?

Answer: By working to resolve conflicts, promoting dialogue and international cooperation, and actively striving for justice and peace.

Conclusion

In concluding the book "1001 Questions and Answers About Christian Life," we would like to emphasize that we have guided our readers through a wide range of topics - from the nature of God, through religious practices, to Christian ethics and the challenges of the modern world. Each question and answer has been a step toward a deeper understanding of our faith and its practices. Through these pages, we have encouraged continuous questioning and seeking answers because dialogue with oneself, with others, and with God is crucial in our spiritual journey.

We remind you that Christianity offers a universal message of love, hope, and compassion that transcends all cultural and national boundaries. May this book serve as an encouragement for your ongoing spiritual and personal development, remembering that the journey of faith is a continuous process of learning, growth, and transformation.

We emphasize the importance of community in Christian life, where the Church not only leads and supports but also creates a space where we can share our faith and experiences. As Christians, we are called to respond to contemporary challenges, and may our faith guide us in working for justice, peace, and the protection of our planet.

Thank you for the time you've dedicated to reading this book; your engagement and openness to exploring matters of faith are highly valued by us. We encourage you not only to contemplate Christian teachings but also to actively incorporate them into your life. May your faith find expression in serving others and in everyday acts of love.

From the depths of our hearts, we bless you on your spiritual journey. May the hope and love flowing from our faith be your guide and a source of strength in each day. Remember, every ending is the beginning of a new path. We encourage you to continue searching, asking questions, and nurturing your faith. May this book be a stop on your wonderful journey of spiritual growth and discoveries. Let this book be a source of inspiration and a guide in your ongoing journey of faith.

www.ingramcontent.com/pod-product-compliance
Lightning Source LLC
LaVergne TN
LVHW012049200726
843506LV00023BA/2570